The *Red Lion* clove through the burning wall as if it were not there. The ship's company felt no heat of its passage. Once on the other side, the magical barrier winked out of existence. The crew gaped with astonishment.

"Just a mirage, an illusion!" roared Conan. "Now muster for boarding, dogs, and we'll see how yon feather-robed sorcerer likes cold steel!"

As the bow of the *Red Lion* came closer and closer to the stern of the galley, those on the carack could see the stern, masklike features of the shaven-skulled magician working with rage. Then he lifted both arms, so that his gorgeous cloak spread in the wind like the blazing pinions of some legendary phoenix.

"Hai, Xotli! Chahuatypak ya-xingoth!" he screamed.

And the Red Shadows struck. . . .

Chronological order of the CONAN series:

Illustrated CONAN novels:

Other CONAN novels:

CONAN
OF THE ISLES

L. Sprague de Camp

and

Lin Carter

SF
ACE BOOKS, NEW YORK

An Ace Book

ISBN: 0-441-11613-2

Tenth Ace Printing: November 1982

Published simultaneously in Canada

Manufactured in the United States of America

Ace Books, 200 Madison Avenue, New York, New York 10016

Contents

Pages 6 and 7: A map of the world of Conan in the Hyborian Age, based upon notes and sketches by Robert E. Howard and upon previous maps by P. Schuyler Miller, John D. Clark, David Kyle, and L. Sprague de Camp, with a map of Europe and adjacent regions superimposed for reference.

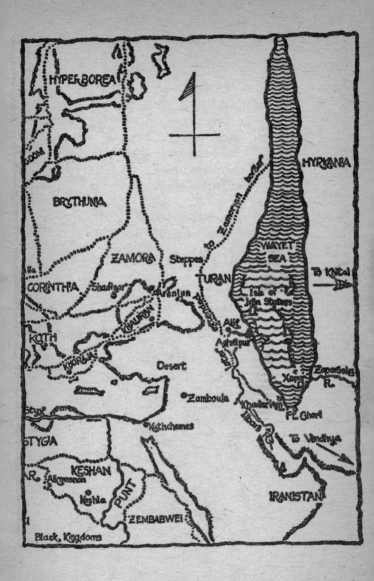

**CONAN
OF THE ISLES**
*is dedicated to
John Jakes,
Fritz Leiber,
Michael Moorcock,
and Jack Vance,*

*our colleagues in S.A.G.A.—
the Swordsmen & Sorcerers'
Guild of America, Ltd.*

Introduction

THERE IS a kind of story laid, not in the world as it is or was, but as—to an armchair adventurer—it *ought* to have been. It is an adventure-fantasy, laid in an imaginary prehistoric or medieval world, where magic works and the scientific revolution has not taken place. Or perhaps it is in some parallel universe, or in this world as it will be in the distant future, when science has been forgotten and magic has revived.

In such a world, gleaming cities raise their shining spires against the stars; sorcerers cast sinister spells from subterranean lairs; baleful spirits stalk crumbling ruins; primeval monsters crash through jungle thickets; and the fate of kingdoms is balanced on bloody broadswords brandished by heroes of preternatural might and valor. In such a world, men are mighty, women are beautiful, life is adventurous, and problems are simple. Nobody even mentions the income tax or the dropout problem or socialized medicine. Such a story is called "heroic fantasy" or, sometimes, "sword-and-sorcery."

The purpose of heroic fantasy is neither to solve the problems of the steel industry, nor to expose defects in the foreign-aid program, nor to expound the questions of poverty or intergroup hostility. It is to entertain. It is escape reading in which one escapes clear out of the real

9

universe. But, come to think, these tales are no more "unreal" than the many whodunnits wherein, after the stupid police have fallen over their own big feet, the brilliant amateur—a private detective, a newspaper reporter, or a little old lady—steps in and solves the crime.

Heroic fantasies combine the color, gore, and lively action of the costume novel with the atavistic terrors and delights of the fairy tale. They furnish the purest *fun* to be found in fiction today. If you read for fun, this is the genre for you.

The heroic fantasy traces its ancestry back to the myths and epics of ancient times—to the stories of Odysseus and Rustam and Sigurd and Cuchulainn. Down the centuries, many civilized writers like Ovid, Firdausi, Geoffrey of Monmouth, Spenser, and James Stephens have collected these tales, edited or rewritten them, and composed pastiches based upon them.

During the seventeenth and eighteenth centuries, stories of the supernatural were neglected in Europe. Then, however, fantasy reëntered the main stream of Western literature through three channels: the oriental fantasy narrative, which first appeared in the form of Galland's translation into French of the *Arabian Nights*; the Gothic novel, brought from Germany to England by Horace Walpole with his *Castle of Otranto* (1764); and the child's fairy tale, originally based upon the peasant tales written up and popularized by Andersen and the Grimm brothers.

At the same time, Walter Scott launched the modern historical novel with his *Waverly* (1814) and its many successors. Although people had long written stories laid in periods before their own—Homer's *Iliad* is an obvious example—Scott was the first to realize that the past had been drastically different in many ways from the present

10

and that these differences of costume and custom in themselves had entertainment value, which a skilled storyteller could exploit. Scott's novels were so influential that they touched off a wave of British medieval romanticism.

In the 1880s, William Morris, the versatile British artist, decorator, poet, reformer, publisher, and novelist, created the modern heroic fantasy. In his pseudo-medieval novels like *The Well at the World's End*, Morris combined the antiquarian romanticism of Scott and his imitators with the supernaturalism of Walpole and *his* imitators. After Morris, Lord Dunsany adapted heroic fantasy to the short-story form early in the present century, while Eric R. Eddison composed his long Zimiamvian novels in the same genre.

The appearance of the American magazines *Weird Tales* in 1923 and *Unknown Worlds* in 1939 created new markets for heroic fantasy. Many notable tales of swordplay and sorcery appeared in them—notably those of Clark Ashton Smith, Robert E. Howard, C. L. Moore, Henry Kuttner, L. Ron Hubbard, and Fritz Leiber. The market for such fiction shrank after these magazines ceased publication (in 1943 and 1953 respectively) and it looked for a while as if heroic fantasy had become a casualty of the machine age.

Certain trends of the time in mainstream fiction were against heroic fantasy. These included the vogue for stories presenting a strongly subjective, sentimental, or psychological view; stories about an anti-hero—a dull, pathetic little twerp who could do nothing right; stories concealing their lack of an interesting narrative by a pyrotechnic display of stylistic eccentricities; and stories with an intense and absorbing interest in contemporary politics or in sex, especially in its more bizarre manifestations. A lecturer lately has said that, if a fiction writer wants sales, he should write exclusively either about politics or about sex. (A novel called *The President's Boyfriend* ought to be a lead-pipe cinch.)

There are still, however, many readers who read, not to be enlightened, improved, uplifted, reformed, baffled by the writer's obscurity, amazed by his cleverness, nauseated by his scatology, or reduced to tears by the plight of some mistreated person, class, or caste, but to be entertained. To please such readers, heroic fantasy has been revived in recent years. The first sign of this revival was the surprising success of J. R. R. Tolkien's trilogy, *The Lord of the Rings,* which appeared in the middle 1950s.

Of course, to enjoy heroic fantasy, one needs some slight imagination. One must be able to suspend one's disbelief in ghoulies and ghosties and other denizens of the worlds of fantasy. If, however, the reader can believe in international spies who race about in superpowered cars from one posh gambling joint to another and find a beautiful babe awaiting them in bed at each stop, a few dragons and demons ought not to daunt him.

Of all the stalwart heroes of heroic fantasy, the most vigorous, virile, brawny, and mettlesome is Conan the Cimmerian. Conan was the invention of Robert E. Howard (1906–36). Howard was born in Peaster, Texas, and lived most of his life in Cross Plains, in the center of Texas. During his last decade, he turned out a large volume of what was then called "pulp fiction"—sport, detective, western, historical, adventure, weird, and ghost stories, as well as his poetry and his many fantasies. He was influenced by Edgar Rice Burroughs, Robert W. Chambers, Harold Lamb, Jack London, H. P. Lovecraft, Talbot Mundy, and Sax Rohmer among others. At the age of thirty, he ended a promising literary career by suicide.

Although he had his faults as a writer, Howard was a natural storyteller, whose narratives are unmatched for vivid, gripping, headlong action. His heroes—King Kull, Conan, Bran Mak Morn, Solomon Kane—are larger than life: men of mighty thews, hot passions, and indomitable will, who easily dominate the stories through which they stride. In fiction, the difference between a writer who is a natural storyteller and one who is not is like the difference between a boat that will float and one that will not. If the writer has this quality, we can forgive many other faults; if not, no other virtue can make up for the lack, any more than gleaming paint and sparkling brass on a boat make up for the fact that it will not float.

Howard wrote several series of heroic fantasies, most of them published in *Weird Tales*. Of these, the longest single series comprised the Conan stories, which have also proved the most popular. In reading the Conan stories, one gets the illusion that one is listening to the mighty adventurer himself, sitting before a fire and reeling off tales of his exploits.

Eighteen Conan tales, from a 3,000-word short story to a 66,000-word novel, were published in Howard's lifetime. Eight others, from complete manuscripts to mere fragments and outlines, have been discovered among Howard's papers since 1950.

Late in 1951, it was my fortune to find a cache of Howard's manuscripts in the apartment of the then literary agent for Howard's estate. These included a few unpublished Conan stories, which I edited for publication. Other manuscripts have been discovered during the last few years, in other collections of Howard's papers, by Glenn Lord, literary agent for the Howard estate. (Howard seemingly never threw anything away; even his high-school examination papers still exist.)

The obviously incomplete state of the Conan saga has

tempted me and others to add to it, as Howard might have done had he lived. Besides editing the unpublished Conan stories, I undertook, in the early 1950s, to rewrite the manuscripts of four other unpublished Howard adventure stories to convert them into Conan stories. These stories were laid in the Orient in medieval and modern times. The conversion did not prove difficult, since the heroes were all cut from the same cloth as Conan. I had merely to change names, delete anachronisms, and introduce a supernatural element. The stories remained about three-quarters or four-fifths Howard.

Since then, in company with my colleagues Björn Nyberg and Lin Carter, I have been engaged in completing the incomplete Conan stories and in writing several pastiches, based upon hints in Howard's notes and letters, to fill the gaps in the saga. The present story, by Carter and me, is based upon a paragraph in a letter that Howard wrote, three months before his untimely death, to the educator and science-fiction writer P. Schuyler Miller, an old Conan fan. Howard wrote:

[Conan] travelled widely, not only before his kingship, but after he was king. He travelled in Khitai and Hyrkania, and to the even less known regions north of the latter and south of the former. He even visited a nameless continent in the western hemisphere, and roamed among the islands adjacent to it. How much of this roaming will get into print, I cannot foretell with any accuracy . . .
(The entire letter is printed in the volume *Conan*.)

Conan lived, loved, and fought about twelve thousand years ago, eight thousand years after the sinking of Atlantis and seven thousand years before the beginnings of recorded history. In this time (according to Howard) the western parts of the main continent were occupied by the Hyborian kingdoms. These comprised a galaxy of states set up by northern invaders, the Hyborians, three thousand years before on the ruins of the evil empire of Acheron. South of the Hyborian kingdoms lay the quarreling city-states of Shem. Beyond Shem slumbered the ancient, sinister kingdom of Stygia, the rival and partner of Acheron in the days of the latter's bloodstained glory. Further south yet, beyond deserts and veldts, were barbarous black kingdoms.

North of the Hyborians lay the barbarian lands of Cimmeria, Hyperborea, Vanaheim, and Asgard. West, along the ocean, were the fierce Picts. To the east glittered the Hyrkanian kingdoms, of which the mightiest was Turan.

Conan was a gigantic barbarian adventurer who roistered and brawled and battled his way across half the prehistoric world to rise at last to the kingship of a mighty realm. The son of a blacksmith in the bleak, backward northern land of Cimmeria, Conan was born on a battlefield in that land of rugged hills and somber skies. As a youth, he took part in the sack of the Aquilonian frontier post of Venarium.

Subsequently, joining in a raid with a band of Æsir into Hyperborea, Conan was captured by the Hyperboreans. Escaping from the Hyperborean slave pen, he wandered south into the kingdom of Zamora. For several years, he made a precarious living there and in the adjacent lands of Corinthia and Nemedia as a thief. (See the map.) Green to civilization and quite lawless by nature, he made up for his lack of subtlety and sophistication by natural shrewdness and by the herculean physique he had inherited from his father.

Growing tired of this starveling existence, Conan enlisted as a mercenary soldier in the armies of Turan. For the next two years he traveled widely, as far east as the fabled lands of Meru and Khitai. He also refined his archery and horsemanship, both of which had been at best indifferent up to the time of his joining the Turanians.

As a result of a quarrel with a superior officer, Conan left Turan. After an unsuccessful try at treasure-hunting in Zamora and a brief visit to his Cimmerian homeland, he embarked upon the career of a mercenary soldier in the Hyborian kingdoms. Circumstances—violent as usual—made him a pirate along the coasts of Kush, with a crew of black corsairs and the Shemitish she-pirate Bêlit as his partner. The natives called him Amra, the Lion.

After Bêlit was slain, Conan became a chief among the black tribes. Then he served as a *condottiere* in Shem and among the southernmost Hyborian kingdoms. Later still, Conan appeared as a leader of the *kozaki*, a horde of outlaws who roamed the steppes between the Hyborian lands and Turan. He was captain of a pirate craft on the great inland Sea of Vilayet and a chief among the nomadic Zuagirs of the southeastern deserts.

After a stretch as a mercenary captain in the army of the king of Iranistan, Conan arrived in the foothills of the Himelian Mountains, a vast stretch of broken country sundering Iranistan, Turan, and the tropical kingdom of Vendhya. In the course of wild adventures, he tried but failed to weld the fierce hill tribes into a united power. Next, he returned westward for another stretch of soldiering in Koth and Argos. During this period, he was briefly co-ruler of the desert city of Tombalku. Then back to the sea, first as a pirate of the Baracha Isles, then as captain of a ship of the Zingaran buccaneers.

When rival buccaneers sank Conan's ship, he served again as mercenary in Stygia and among the black kingdoms. Then he wandered north to Aquilonia and became a scout on the Pictish frontier. When the Picts, with the help of the wizard Zogar Sag, attacked the Aquilonian settlements, Conan failed to save Fort Tuscelan but did save the lives of a number of settlers between the Thunder and Black rivers.

After rising to command in the Aquilonian army and defeating a Pictish invasion, Conan was lured back to Tarantia, the capital, and imprisoned by the jealous King Numedides. Escaping, he became involved in a three-cornered conflict among the Picts and two crews of pirates on the western coast of Pictland. Then he was chosen to lead an Aquilonian revolution against the degenerate King Numedides. Slaying Numedides on his own throne, Conan, in his early forties, became the ruler of the mightiest Hyborian kingdom.

Conan soon found that being king was no bed of houris. A cabal of discontented nobles almost succeeded in assassinating him. By a ruse, the kings of Ophir and Koth trapped and imprisoned him in order to have a free hand with the conquest of Aquilonia. With the help of a fellow prisoner—a wizard—Conan escaped in time to turn the tables on the invaders.

Subsequently, a cabal of rivals plotting to gain the rule of Aquilonia revived the mummy of a long-dead Acherontian wizard, Xaltotun, to aid them in their enterprise. Conan was defeated and driven from his kingdom, but again he returned to confound his foes.

In the process, Conan for the first time acquired a legitimate queen. This was Zenobia, a slave girl who saved his life when he was imprisoned in the dungeon under the palace of King Tarascus of Nemedia. He tactfully dismissed his harem of shapely concubines and settled down to the pleasures and pains of wedded life. A Khitan sorcerer kidnapped Zenobia, forcing Conan to travel across half the world, through manifold perils, to recover her. Other plots and adventures involved Conan and his young son, also named Conan but usually known by his nickname of ''Conn.''

Time passed; Zenobia died. Conan found his son nearing maturity and old age creeping upon himself. A growing restlessness perturbed and irritated him . . .

L. SPRAGUE DE CAMP

"—And at the last, O Prince, there came to pass that which all the plots of Ascalante the Rebel had failed to bring about, and for which the grim shade of Xaltotun was conjured in vain from the mouldering dust of his Acherontic tomb, and which even the hell-spawned sorceries of Yah Chieng, the Yellow Wizard of nighted and demon-ridden Khitai, failed to accomplish; and Conan of Aquilonia gave over the crown and the throne of the mightiest kingdom of all the West, and ventured forth into the Unknown, wherein he vanished forever from the knowledge of man."

—THE NEMEDIAN CHRONICLES

After the events described in the volume Conan of Aquilonia, Conan's rule is for several years relatively peaceful. His old foes Thoth-Amon and King Yezdigerd are no more, and turbulent Zingara has been reduced to a quiet client kingdom under the rule of Conan's docile puppet. The savage Picts resent and resist the constant pressure against their forest fastness, but that is to be expected.

The event of these years that most affects Conan is the death of his queen, Zenobia, in childbirth. Thereafter, Conan finds the routine of a peaceful reign increasingly irksome. He haunts the royal library, finding in dusty scrolls and crumbling codices strange accounts of lands beyond the Western Ocean. He spends time with his children, but the yawning gap in age—he is in his sixties, while they are still infants and adolescents—makes it hard for him to reach any true intimacy with them. And then a sudden catastrophe shatters his mood of vague, half-resigned discontent . . .

1. Red Shadows

> From gulfs profound wherein yet dwell age-old,
> forgotten, nameless things,
> The Shadows came on silent wings as crimson
> as the heart of Hell.
>   —*The Visions of Epemitreus*

KING CONAN sat on the judgment throne in the Hall of Justice in his palace at Tarantia, the royal capital of Aquilonia. Beyond windows of stained glass, blue skies curved over green gardens bright and fragrant with blossoms. And beyond the gardens, square towers of white stone thrust into the sky, and domes of green copper, and the shapes of houses, temples, and palaces roofed with red tiles. For this was the most princely city of the world's West in these ancient days of the Hyborian Age.

And beyond the gardens, too, the well-scrubbed streets of Tarantia swarmed with traffic: men and women afoot, on the backs of horses, mules, and asses, in litters and chariots and oxcarts and carriages. Along the waterfront, river boats plied the Khorotas like swarms of water insects. For two decades of the firm but tolerant rule of Conan the Great had made Aquilonia not only the most powerful but also the most prosperous land which that dawn world had ever seen.

Within the pillared hall richly clad nobles, silken courtiers, and stout burghers in plain cloth, with the medallions of the guilds on silver chains about their necks, stood in clusters while the king dispensed justice. Since the docket carried some cases of exceptional importance, half the high-born of Aquilonia were here. They included young Gonzalvio, Viscount of Poitain, and his father, old Trocero, slim and elegant as ever in scarlet velvet, with the golden leopard of his province broidered in stiff, silvergilt wire on the breast of his jupon. Here, too, were Count Monargo of Couthen, Baron Guilaime of Imirus, and—a lean, snowy-bearded ancient—the wise and learned Dexitheus, Archpriest of Mitra.

Grim-faced warriors of the king's black-mailed legions stood at arched door and portico, the sunlight flashing from their dragon-crested helms and glittering spear points. All eyes were fixed upon the central dais, where two thrones loomed above the throng; and upon the fat, bejeweled merchant who stood, fidgeting nervously, as his advocate in robes of dusty black glibly argued on his behalf before the taller of the two thrones.

On the throne, Conan glowered down upon the quivering litigant. From the depths of his soul he loathed these tiresome, wordy, labyrinthine tax cases, with their plausible lies and their mathematical calculations of skull-cracking complexity. How he would have liked to hurl his crown at the fat face of the greedy fool before him, stride from the hall, clamp his legs about a stallion's barrel, and ride off for a day's hunting in the forests of the North!

A pox upon this business of kinging it! he thought. It drained every last drop of juice from a man's tissues, leaving him a querulous old hairsplitter without enough red blood in his veins to swing a broadsword. Surely, after twenty weary years of wearing the crown, a man was en-

22

titled to throw over honors and titles and set out toward dim horizons for one last, gore-spattered adventure before Time's all-felling, implacable scythe cut him down . . .

Conan stole a glance at the second throne, whereon sat his son, Prince Conn, the heir of Aquilonia. The lad was twenty—old enough, surely, to take the throne of the mightiest kingdom of the West. With a slight smile on his grim lips, the old king studied the bored, mutinous glower of dissatisfaction on the face of young Conn. Doubtless the lad was also dreaming of flinging off these stifling robes of state and riding off for a day's hunting, or perhaps a night of wenching in waterfront dives. Remembering his own hard-drinking, hot-blooded youth, Conan chuckled.

In truth, Prince Conn was the very image of his sire in his younger days: the same scowling black brows over deep-set eyes of volcanic blue; the same swart, square-jawed face, framed by a square-cut mane of straight, coarse black hair; the same burly blacksmith's body, sheathed in massive muscles that bulged the silks and velvets at the broad shoulders and deep-arched chest; the same long, steel-thewed legs. Scarce out of his teens, the son of Conan towered head and shoulders over most of the men in the hall, save only his titanic sire, the greatest warrior the world had ever known.

As for King Conan, even that mightiest of champions, Time, had not yet broken him. True, sixty-odd years had strewn abundant silver in the thick, black mane and the stiff, grizzled beard, cut short and square, that now clothed his grim lips and iron jaw. Some flesh had fallen from his mighty frame, leaving him gaunt as a savage gray wolf of the northern steppes. And Time's cold hand had etched deep grooves in his somber brow and scarred cheeks.

But still unquenchable vitality surged within his titanic form. Hot flames of leashed fury smouldered in his eyes. And Time's palsying grip had sapped but little of the strength from his viselike hands—now wrinkled and corded—and his supple sinews and massive thews.

He sat on the silver throne as if he bestrode some deep-chested war stallion on the foughten field. One massive hand gripped the black-and-silver mace of justice as if it were an iron-spiked battle mace that he would heave up at any moment to strike down a foe. And the rich robes, crusted with gems and hung with golden medallions and chains, which clothed his lean but mighty form, bore somehow the look of battle harness. For wherever he went—in mirthful banquet hall, in quiet library of ancient, dusty tones, or in silken boudoir—this somber barbarian from the cloud-cloaked wastes of northern Cimmeria carried with him the grim, dangerous atmosphere of the battle-field.

It had been more than a score of years now since a trick of Fate, a whim of the gods, or perhaps his own indomitable will had lifted this black-browed outlander from the ranks of nameless adventurers to a glittering place among the great ones of the world as lord of the richest and most powerful kingdom of the West. Since that night, nearly half a century before, when as a ragged, wild-eyed youth, whirling a length of broken chain, he had fought his way out of a Hyborian slave pen and set forth barehanded on the road that leads but a chosen few to the ultimate heights of power and glory, Conan of Cimmeria had brawled and battled his way across half a world, cutting a red path through a dozen kingdoms from the thundering beaches of the Western Ocean to the misty vales of fabulous Khitai.

As thief, pirate, mercenary, adventurer, chief of barbarous tribes, and general in the armies of kings, he had ventured far and known all that the world afforded of adventure and marvel. With his irresistible sword, the mighty Cimmerian had fought demons, dragons, and

24

shambling horrors of the Elder Dark. A thousand foes had felt the bitter kiss of his whirling blade—bronze-mailed warriors, malevolent wizards, fierce barbarian chieftains, and haughty kings. Even the eternal gods had sometimes fled the fury of his slashing brand.

But the adventure that started here, in the royal Hall of Justice in Tarantia, on this warm spring day, eight thousand years after the fall of Atlantis and seven thousand years before the rise of Egypt and Sumeria, was to be the strangest and most fantastic of all the many that thronged his far-famed and peril-filled career.

It began suddenly and unexpectedly.

One moment, Conan was frowning down upon the fat merchant and his glib, gesticulating advocate. The next, he raised a puzzled glance across the hall to where the elegant figure of his trusted old friend, Count Trocero of Poitain, staggered across the polished floor.

"No, no! By all the scarlet fiends of Hell!"

The old nobleman's hoarse voice, lifted in harsh tones of terror and despair, broke into the advocate's voluble pleadings. Startled eyes flashed to his stiff-legged, reeling figure. Eyebrows rose. Could it be that the old Count of Poitain had come into the Hall of Justice *drunk*?

One look at the stark fear in Trocero's bloodless face banished that idea. Globules of cold sweat glistened on his white features, and his pallid lips worked as if in some inward agony. Black circles ringed his staring eyes.

"Trocero!" barked Conan. "Are you unwell? What is it, man?"

The king half rose as his oldest friend and closest supporter reeled across the polished marble pave, arms thrust out as if to ward off some unseen attacker. The hall fell silent. Trocero's stalwart son started from the throng, one hand extended to support his sire. In the center of the hall, Trocero halted and stood on trembling limbs, crying:

"Nay, I say! I cannot—you *dare* not! Oh, Ishtar and Mitra! *Mit*—" His voice rose to a screech of anguish.

And then Terror struck.

From the groined and vaulted ceiling above the corners of the spacious hall, shadows flew—shadows as pale and insubstantial as wisps of gauze, dimly red. Shadows of—Terror.

In the blink of an eye, they swarmed about the elderly Poitanian's tottering figure. Dimly through rubescent veils, the others in the hall could glimpse his white, frozen features, fixed in a grimace of torment. It was as if a horde of ghostly vampire bats had swooped to cling about the unwary traveler.

For a long, frozen moment, the red shadows enveloped their victim in rosy veils. Then they and he were gone.

The hall was a motionless tableau. Disbelief was stamped on every face. The old count of Poitain, who for a quarter-century had stood by Conan's throne and fought his wars, had vanished into thin air.

"Father! My Lord—" stammered young Gonzalvio into the ringing silence.

"By Crom's iron heart!" bellowed Conan. "Black sorcery in my own court? I'll have the head of him who wrought this mischief! Ho, guard! Curse you for a gaping fool—sound the alarm!"

Conan's roar of rage shattered the fragile silence. Women shrieked and swooned. Men swore, rubbed their eyes, and stared blankly at the place where the greatest peer of Aquilonia had stood. Above the babble rose the brazen scream of the war horns. Drums thundered, and the grim-faced warriors of Conan's Black Dragons pushed through the milling confusion, swords in hand, to defend the Lion Banner of Aquilonia, which hung like a canopy over the dais, and the rulers beneath it. But there was no foe to smite: no sly assassin, no skulking spy—or at least none visible.

On the dais, surrounded by his mailed warriors, King Conan searched the hall with the fierce, unwinking gaze of some kingly lion of the veldt. Deep within him, pain lanced his secret heart and a poignant sense of loss assailed him. Trocero of Poitain had been the first to urge Conan's name as leader of the revolt against the degenerate King Numedides. He had led a voyage to the distant shores of Pictland to fetch back the former general of the armies of Aquilonia, then a fugitive from the murderous jealousy of Numedides.

Soon, Conan had ridden out of Zingara at the head of a handful of gallant warriors. Gathering partisans as he moved, he had cut like a red sword through the countryside of Aquilonia to the gates of tower-crowned Tarantia and then to the very steps of the throne. There he had throttled the depraved Numedides with his own hands and set the crown upon his own black head. Deep within him, Conan mourned the loss of his oldest and most trusted friend, the first victim of the Terror . . .

In the next halfmonth, the Terror struck again and again, until seven hundred citizens of Aquilonia—peer and porter, countess and courtezan, baron and beggar, priest and peasant—had vanished into the weird embrace of the red shadows.

II. The Black Heart of Golamira

Whilst age on age went rolling past beyond
   my phoenix-guarded tomb,
In silent halls of somber gloom I slept,
   but now I wake at last.
                —*The Visions of Epemitreus*

ALONE AND closely guarded in the great, gold-domed chamber of his palace, Conan slept. It was a haunted, restless slumber, for all that he had not slept a single hour in the last three days and nights while he struggled to cope with the weird plague that gripped his kingdom. Through desperate days and nights of endless council, he had sought the advice of the wisest men of the kingdom—hoary sages and learned doctors. He had asked the prayers of the priests of Mitra and Ishtar and Asura. He had listened to the tales of spies and studied the reports of police agents. He had solicited the spells and divinations of wizards and occultists—all in vain.

Now exhaustion had sapped even his iron vigor. The gray, gaunt old wolf lay sprawled in chain mail upon the silken coverlets, his great broadsword near his hand, in a drugged but restless slumber.

And in this sleep, he dreamed.

It seemed to Conan that he heard a distant voice. The echoing call was loud enough to rouse him but so fogged and unclear that he could not understand the repeated phrase that whispered eerily through his chamber.

He came to his feet, saw that his mighty limbs were bare, and knew that it was but a dream. Looking back, he saw his own body lying deep in slumber. As the deep chest rose and fell, mail glinted like silver in the moonlight that shone through the tall narrow windows.

Again came that distant, murmuring call, and the note of urgency rang within it. And in a fashion he could never quite remember afterwards, the old king went forward from the moonlit darkness of his chamber, through barriers of space and time, until swirling mists as gray as his own grizzled beard closed about him, blotting everything from sight. Yet still he advanced, in some form of progress unlike the ways of the material world he had left behind—forward, through grayness that obscured his vision like the clammy embrace of a night-born fog.

Out of the shifting mists came, again and again, that haunting call that had summoned his spirit forth from its mansion of flesh and into this world of eery darkness and phantom mists. Gradually the call of the voice, repeated over and over, became clearer: "Conan of Cimmeria!—Conan of Aquilonia!—Conan of the Isles!"

Yes, he could hear it distinctly now. But he was puzzled: what meant the name "Conan of the Isles"? Never had this term been linked with his name in all the wide-ranging years of his wanderings.

Now he came to where he could stand on a solid footing. And it seemed, in his dream, that the gray fog cleared away. A dim, unearthly light struck through the blur of vapor. Now he stood in a hall of titanic proportions, whose ebon walls and lofty, vaulted roof seemed carved from the dead-black stuff of Old Night itself. The faint, mystic radiance seemed to shine from the very walls themselves, whereon he could dimly discern colossal carvings, which stretched from the floor to the arched ceiling far above.

Every inch of the black walls was cut and worked into a stupendous pageant of tiny figures—a vast, sweeping panorama peopled with millions of struggling, warring men. Peering closer, he marveled vaguely at the strangeness of their raiment and weaponry, derived from distant realms and remote aeons.

It was like a titanic tapestry of cold stone, a bird's-eye view of the history of man himself, from the forgotten days before the Cataclysm, when Atlantis and Lemuria, Valusia and old Grondar strove for the mastery of the earth; and even earlier, when the stooped and hairy ancestors of men slouched through the jungle, and black-winged Ka, the Bird of Creation, first flew out of the unknown East to lay the foundations of Time.

Above this straggling pageant of ancient kings and heroes loomed other shapes as well—malformed, uncouth, and terrible. In his soul, Conan knew them for the Nameless Old Ones, who had ruled the star-thronged universe a billion aeons before the birth of Gayomar the First of All Men.

Then Conan knew that he walked through a timeless dream, wherein his spirit had been summoned by an ancient Force which guarded and watched over the race of man. With an inward queasiness natural to his blunt, barbaric soul, he knew that the foot of mortal man had not stirred the impalpable dust that filmed this ebon floor for ages beyond reckoning. Aye, he knew all this and more, for once in earlier years he had stood upon this very spot and passed down the yawning black throat of this colossal hall in a strange, magical dream.

More than a score of years had passed since that distant day, but what are the ephemeral generations of mortal men to him who sleeps forever in the black halls of timeless Golamira, the Mount of Eternal Time?

Conan came upon a broad, curving stair, which rose in steep ramps of black stone to unguessable heights. Here, the cliff-like walls were adorned with cryptic symbols in some esoteric script, so ancient and so suggestive that they woke within him vestigial memories inherited from ancestors scarce risen above the primal, shambling beastmen of Time's dawn. And at the stir of these racial memories of Elder Time, the skin seemed to crawl on his naked flanks. He hastily averted his eyes from these enigmatic glyphs.

As he went up the mighty stair, he saw that every step was carven with the writhing coils of that abhorrent form of nightmare, Set the Old Serpent, eternal and malignant Demon of Darkness, in such a manner that with every stride he set his heel upon the blunt, questing serpent-head that lifted from the fluid, scaly neck. This the unknown builders had meant the wayfarer to do, in symbolic refutation of the forces of blind, evil chaos. Step by step, Conan mounted the curving stair.

At last he saw the tomb itself, hewn from one massive, glittering crystal that he could not name. If it were diamond—as in truth it seemed—then the gem whence the tomb was wrought had been vast beyond calculation. The cold crystal glittered with a thousand points of restless light, like a multitude of captive stars.

To either side, in the silent gloom of the nighted crypt, rose the terrible forms of two stupendous phoenixes, clawed and beaked, with wings outspread as if to shelter beneath their stony pinions him who slept within the diamond sepulcher.

From the ebon gloom emerged a titanic figure, robed and haloed in purest light. Conan stared silently into the majestic, bearded face.

"Speak, O mortal!" the face commanded, in a deep voice as resonant as trumpets. "Know you who I am?"

"Aye," growled Conan. "By Crom and Mitra and all the gods of light, you are the prophet Epemitreus, whose flesh has been moldering dust these fifteen hundred years!"

"True, O Conan. It has been many years since last I summoned your sleeping spirit to stand before me here in the black heart of Golamira. In the years gone by since that day, my undying sight has followed you through all your wandering ways and wars across the earth, and it is well. All has been done as the Eternal Ones who set me here as man's guardian would wish. But now a darkness hovers over all the lands of the West—a Shadow that you alone of all mortal men can dispel."

Conan started at these unexpected words and would have spoken, but the bony hand of the ancient sage lifted, commanding silence.

"Harken well, O Conan! In olden time, the Lords of Life gave me powers and wisdom beyond those granted to other men, that I might wage war against the infernal and malignant Serpent, old Set, whom I strove against and slew, and in the slaughter gained my own death as well. These things you know."

"So the old books and legends tell," Conan growled.

"And so it was." The radiant figure nodded. "You know, O child of man, that from the beginning the gods of eternity marked you for great deeds and undying fame, and many and perilous have been the grim dangers through which your path has led, and many dark and evil men and superhuman forces have gone down before your sword. And the gods are pleased."

His grim face impassive, Conan made no reply to this praise. After a pause, the deep, ringing voice of Epemitreus spoke on.

"One last task awaits you, O Cimmerian, ere you may go to your well-earned rest. For this task, your spirit was

32

destined from before the beginning of time itself. One last and Mightiest victory awaits you—but the price to be paid is a bitter one."

"What is the task, and what the price?" bluntly demanded Conan.

"The task is to save the West of the world from the Terror that even now stalks your green land. A terrible doom hovers over the lands of men, a doom darker than your mind can grasp—a Terror that strikes down and enslaves the very souls of your people, whilst their poor bodies are rent asunder in hideous and bestial torment by hands that should have fallen into dust eight thousand years ago!"

The prophet fixed Conan's sullen face with the splendor of his blazing eyes.

"But, to accomplish this, you needs must render up your throne and kingly crown to your son and venture forth alone to the dim horizons of the uttermost reaches of the Western Ocean, where never mortal man of your race has ventured since doomed Atlantis sank beneath the glittering waves. This very night must you set forth alone from your kingdom, in stealth and secrecy, never more to gaze upon it in the flesh, leaving behind your crown and realm and a writ of abdication.

"The way into the unknown seas is long and hard, and many perils stand between you and your ultimate goal—perils whence not even the gods can shield you. But only you, of all men, can treat that path with a chance of victory. Yours alone are the perils and the glory; for it is given to few mortals to save their world!"

The sage smiled down at the king from the cloudy light. "One gift alone I may give you. Bear it through every trial, for in your hour of greatest need it will be your salvation. Nay, I can tell you naught more. In time of need, your heart will instruct you how to use this talisman."

A mist of glittering light, like the dust of stars, drifted

from the prophet's outstretched palm. Something tinkled glassily at Conan's feet. Without looking, he bent to pick it up.

"One last word," said Epemitreus. "The sorcerer-kings of old Atlantis used the emblem of the Black Kraken. This emblem is still displayed. Beware of it!

"Go now, child of Crom," continued the sage. "It were not wise for mortals to stray too long into these shadowy realms whereinto I have called your spirit. Return, O Conan, to your fleshly abode, and the blessing of the eternal gods of light go with you, to lighten your dark and dreadful path! Never again shall you behold the face of Epemitreus—not in this world, nor yet in the many worlds to come, through which your soul, reborn, shall venture and struggle in lives beyond this one. Farewell!"

Gasping with shock, Conan came instantly awake. He found himself sprawled on the silken bed, clad in light mail and bathed in sweat. So it had been a dream! The drugged wine and his own troubled thoughts had combined to form a fearful vision . . .

And then he looked at the thing clenched in his sweaty palm, the phoenix-shaped talisman hewn from the heart of a giant, glittering diamond, and knew that it had been more than a mere dream.

Three hours later, while a drenching summer storm flashed and rumbled about the towers of the palace, a giant, mail-clad form swathed in a vast black cloak and with its face half hidden by a wide-brimmed black slouch hat stole forth from the little-used secret sally port in Tarantia's outer wall. After it came another tall, hulking figure, leading a mettlesome stallion. They halted while the second man tested the girth and checked the length of the stirrups.

"Curse it!" growled Prince Conn's young voice. " 'Tis unfair! If any man has the right to go with you, it is I!"

34

Conan somberly shook his head, scattering drops of water from his hat brim. "Crom knows, son, that if I might take any man with me, it would be you. But we are no mere pair of penniless adventurers, to do as the whim moves us. We cannot have the power and the glory without the responsibility. It took me years to learn this lesson, and a hard one at times I found it. I go, perchance to my death; you shall remain to rule this land as justly as you can. Thus the gods have willed.

"Trust no man fully, but give the most trust to those whom I have found worthy of trust. Discount all praise by nine-tenths, since a king draws flatterers as offal does flies. Pay closer heed to men's deeds than to their words. Never punish the bearer of bad tidings, or frown upon him who submits an unwelcome opinion, lest men think they dare not tell the king the truth. Farewell!"

Conan grasped his son's hand in a crushing grip, and the two exchanged a short, fierce hug. Then, while Conn held the stallion's reins and the nigh stirrup, Conan swung into the saddle. For a few heartbeats, the cloaked figure looked back at the looming towers of golden Tarantia, starry gem of the West. Then, with a final wave, Conan spurred the horse southward and rode off through the pouring rain and the lightning-litten dark down the long road to Argos and the sea. And thus the world's mightiest warrior set forth upon the last and strangest of his adventures.

III. The Cup and Trident

Tall thrones topple and kingdoms fall,
And the shuddering dark envelops all;
But one rides forth on a hopeless quest
To a nameless fate in the dim, red West.
                    —*The Voyage of Amra*

THE STORM broke about midnight. Lightning flickered and flared in the thick-piled clouds above the western horizon and ere long a wind rose like a pack of howling wolves, driving sheets of rain before it.

But within the Cup and Trident, a seaside inn near the harbor of Messantia in Argos, all was warmth and light and merriment. A mighty fire roared on the stone hearth, filling the long, low-ceilinged room with flickering orange light and steamy heat. Sailors, fishermen, and an occasional traveler caught by the cloudburst sprawled on log benches before long tables, swilling sour Argossean ale or, for those who could afford a finer liquor, rich Zingaran wine. A bull calf turned on the creaking spit above the roaring blaze, and the spicy smell of roasting meat filled the air.

Caught by the gusty wind, the oaken door crashed open.

36

Men turned, startled, to see a gigantic figure looming in the door. From throat to heel he was wrapped in a black cloak. Streams of water trickled from him, forming puddles on the floor. Under the black, wide-brimmed, wayfarer's hat, the men in the tavern glimpsed dangerous blue eyes in a bronzed, weatherbeaten face and the silver of a hoary beard as the stranger stamped in, slamming the door shut behind him and doffing his voluminous cloak to wring the water from it in streams.

A fat, perspiring innkeeper with a round, red face framed in greasy black curls clumped over to ask the stranger's fancy. He made jerky little bows while rubbing his fat hands on the leathern apron about his paunch.

"Hot mulled ale," the fierce-eyed oldster growled, as he sat down at the bench nearest to the fire. "And a haunch of that calf I smell sizzling, if 'tis done. Quick, man! I'm wet to the bone, frozen to the marrow, and hungry as a famished wolf!"

As the innkeeper puffed away to serve the stranger, a burly, tawny-haired Argossean, much the worse for wine, nudged his comrades and rose to his feet to stand before the fire, rocking a little on his heels. He was big and beefy, with the thickly corded throat and broad, bulging shoulders of a wrestler. The piglike little blue eyes in his round, red face bore an expression of brute cunning and oafish stupidity. He stood looking down with an open, wet-mouthed grin at the old man, taking in the gray mane and the scarred cheeks. Conan, spreading his cloak to catch the heat of the fire, paid him no heed.

"What have we here, lads, eh?" said the red-faced one in a thick voice.

"Looks like a Zingaran buccaneer to me, Strabo," said one of his cronies.

Strabo looked the stranger up and down. "Long in the tooth for a buccaneer, lads," he sneered. "And look at the old dog sitting there, hogging the best seat in the Cup and

Trident! Hey, graybeard! Drag your old bones to the back and let honest Argosseans soak up some heat!"

Conan raised blazing eyes. If Strabo had not been so deep in his cups and spoiling for a fight, the banked fires behind that gaze might have penetrated even his dull wits. As it was, Conan's ominous warning glare only roused him to pettish fury. Childish rage flared in his bloodshot eyes, and his porcine face flushed.

"I'm talking to you, gaffer!" he snarled, and swung one leg to kick Conan's shin with a heavy thud—startlingly loud in the inn, which had become suddenly quiet. This was the local bully, the strong man, the braggart. The other locals chuckled and nudged one another, waiting for the fun when Strabo goaded the old fellow into a rage.

At the other end of the room sat a silent, catlike figure in a shadowy corner, enveloped in a thick, black cloak with the hood drawn close about his face. He leaned forward with strange interest, eyes narrowing to observe the quarrel.

Conan moved like a striking tiger. One moment he sat folded under his steaming cloak; the next, he flashed into a blur of action. As he surged to his feet, one huge, bony, mottled hand clamped like a vise on Strabo's fleshy thigh; the other caught the bully's throat with throttling force. Then Conan, incredibly, swung the heavy Strabo off his feet and hurled him clear across the room. Strabo's body struck the wooden wall with an impact that shook the house and thudded to the plank floor, where he sprawled in a daze. For a moment he lay, gasping. A voice among the onlookers muttered:

"An old dotard like that? Imposs—"

Then Strabo, his face an even brighter scarlet, lurched to his feet. Roaring an incoherent oath, he charged across the room with thick arms outstretched.

Conan stepped forward to meet him. Like a ball of iron, his left fist sank into the other's bulging belly. The air whistled from Strabo's lips, and his face went mottled and gray as tallow. Then, as he doubled over, Conan's right fist caught him in the face with a smack that made men wince. The punch snapped the bully's head back and lifted him clear of the floor. As he came down in a heap, Conan booted him into the fire.

Coals flew and soot shot out in a black cloud. Squealing with alarm, Strabo's comrades rushed to drag the victim—blackened, singed, and grease-spattered—out of the fireplace. They slapped his pale cheeks, but his head merely swayed limply at each blow. Blood from his smashed nose and cut lips ran down over his chin and soaked his doublet. Conan paid no attention as, muttering curses, they bore their unconscious champion to another room for revival.

The tension broke with a chorus of guffaws, congratulations, and compliments on Conan's prowess, for many of those present had long hoped that somebody would some day take the overbearing bully's measure. Conan merely gave a grim little half-smile and addressed himself to the hot mulled ale being served him. Just as he was heartily quaffing the first steaming flagon, a thunderous bellow arrested his attention.

"By the Hammer of Thor and the Fires of Baal, there's only one mortal man in thirty kingdoms could heave yon fat blusterer across the room like that! Is it—can it be—?"

The crowd parted like water before a ship's stem as a towering giant, with a beard of blazing red-gold shot with silver, pushed through. He swaggered up to Conan like a burly crimson bear, magnificent in gold-braided scarlet coat, with a plumed hat set rakishly on his bald head. Golden earrings dangled from his ear lobes. Around his massive belly, a triple length of gorgeous silk was wrapped to form a sash, and thrust into the glittering stuff were a brace of gemmed dirks and an iron-bound cudgel that could brain an ox. A heavy cutlass hung from a gold-worked baldric across his deep chest, and boots of fine Kordavan leather clad his fat bow-legs.

Conan caught a glimpse of a sweaty red face with keen blue eyes twinkling under tufted, rust-colored brows, and the white crescent of a broad grin amidst the fiery bush of bristling beard. He lifted his voice in a bellow of joy.

"Sigurd of Vanaheim, you fat old walrus! By the scarlet bowels of Hell—Sigurd Redbeard!" he roared, rising to clasp the burly seaman in his arms.

"Amra of the *Red Lion*!" cried Sigurd.

"Hush; hold your tongue, you old barrel of whale blubber!" growled Conan. "I've reasons to remain nameless for the while."

"Oh," said Sigurd. In a lower voice he continued: "By the breasts of Badb and the claws of Nergal, broil my guts if it don't warm an old seaman's heart to clap eyes on you!"

They hugged each other like angry bears, then drew apart to pummel each other on the shoulders with buffets that would have sent lesser men staggering.

"Sigurd, by Crom! Sit and drink with me, you barnacled old whale!" Conan roared. The other collapsed, wheezing, on the bench across from the Cimmerian. He doffed his plumed hat and stretched fat legs with a gusty sign.

"Taverner!" boomed Conan. "Another cup, and where's that cursed roast?"

"By Mitra's golden sword and Wodun's league-long spear, ye haven't changed a mite in thirty years!" said the red-bearded Vanr when they had toasted each other. He dragged one crimson cuff across bristling lips and emitted a mighty belch.

"Haven't I, you lying old rogue?" Conan chuckled. "Why, thirty years ago, when I hit a man in the face like that, I broke his jaw and sometimes his neck as well." He sighed. "But old man Time hunts us all down at the last.

40

You've changed, too, Sigurd; that fat gut was as slim as a topsail yard when last we met. Remember how we were becalmed off the Nameless Isle, with naught to eat but the rats in the hold and what few stinking fish we could dredge out of Manannan's wet lair?"

"Aye, aye," the other chuckled, wiping sentimental tears from his eye. "Oh, damn me guts, of course ye've changed, old Lion! They was no silver in your black mane then . . . aye, aye, we were both young and full o' juice in those far days. But sink me! Didn't I hear from one of the Brotherhood that ye were kinging it over some inland realm or other? Corinthia or Brythunia? I misremember which. But by the jaws of Moloch and the green whiskers of Lir, it warms me to see you again, after all these years!"

Over hot beef and more mulled ale, the two comrades exchanged stories. Years before, when Conan had been a member of the Red Brotherhood of the Barachan Isles, the archipelago southwest of the Zingaran coast, he and the red-bearded Vanr had been great friends. Their trails had long since parted, but it was like strong wine to the Cimmerian's lonely soul to meet his old comrade again and swap jests and reminiscences once more before a roaring blaze, with plenty to eat and drink. Now, Conan was winding up his tale.

"So when I woke and saw it was no dream," he growled in a low voice, "I scrawled a writ of abdication in favor of my son, who will rule as Conan the Second, by Crom! There was naught to hold me in Tarantia. Twenty years of ruling leave a sour taste of law-making and treaty-haggling in a man's mouth. I long ago threw down whatever neighboring kings were minded to pick a quarrel with me. Since the fall of the Black Adepts, there's been no real fighting; and a man can get sick of peace and plenty, after a lifetime of red war."

For a moment, Conan brooded with glowering eyes, as if he saw the past unreeled before him. "Ah, true," he sighed. "Aquilonia is fair and green, and I've tried to be a good king to it. But my old friends are gone now: old Publius, the chancellor, who could make three gold pieces sprout where one was sown; Trocero, who helped me to my throne, Pallantides, the general, who always knew what the enemy was thinking even before the enemy himself did. All dead and gone. And since my lass, Zenobia, died giving me a daughter, the very air of Tarantia has grown stale."

He snorted and tossed down a gulp of ale. "It was all right while the lad was young; I took joy in teaching him the use of bow and sword and spear, and horse and chariot. But he's grown now and should be about his own life without the specter of a grumbling old graybeard hovering behind him. I didn't need Epemitreus to tell me. 'Twas time I cleared out for one last adventure. Crom, but I have always dreaded the thought of dying in bed, surrounded by whispering physicians and scurrying courtiers! One last battlefield whereon to fight and fall— that's all I ask of the gods."

"Aye, aye," the burly redbeard agreed with a wheezing sigh, wagging his head so that the firelight glinted from the golden hoops in his ears. " 'Twas much the same with me, Lion, though I never got a crown or a kingdom from the hands of Fate. Nay, I left the Trade years ago—ran a merchantman between Messantia and Kordava. Can ye imagine old Sigurd Redbeard, the terror of Baracha, a *merchant*?" His belly quivered with laughter.

"Ah, and that's not the worst of it, either. Like you, Lion, I settled down with a wench—a fine woman, too, even if she had more than a drop of Pictish blood in her veins. Well, we raised a crop of squalling brats, and now the boys are as big as I am. She's gone years ago, aye, Frigga bless her stout heart, and the younglings grown and thriving on their own. What's to do with old men who will not die, eh?

"Ho! I sold everything when the last child wed. Now I'm on my way back to red, roaring Tortage for one last taste of the old life before the long night sets in. What about you, Lion? Come with me, man, back to the pirate deck, and let take these ghostly prophecies and spectral dooms! Let's sack black-walled Khemi in Stygia! Sink me for a lubber, but either we shall get a spear in the guts and go out like heroes in the sagas, or we shall grab more golden loot than Tranicos, Zarono, and Strombanni rolled into one! Eh, what say ye, man?"

A black shadow fell between them. Conan looked up, one hand going to his sword hilt as the black-cloaked stranger who had been watching them from across the room eased himself into a seat at their table.

"Do you seek a ship, gentlemen?" he said in a purring voice. The Northman rumbled with suspicion, but the cat-like stranger, whose face was still concealed in his hood, placed both gloved hands upon the table, clear of any weapons.

"I could not but help overhear some of your talk," the intruder said smoothly. "Pray forgive this intrusion, but if you will spare me a few moments, I think we can discuss business to our mutual advantage."

Sigurd eyed him dubiously but grunted with curiosity. Conan fixed the man with a level, noncommittal stare. "Speak up, then," he growled. "Say your piece."

The other nodded with a polite half-bow. "Unless I misunderstood the little I overheard, I believe that both of you are old seamen, now thinking of taking ship and resuming a career out of the—ah—Pirate Isles? No, fear not." He raised a placating hand. "I am no spying informer, no police agent—but I may be able to finance you in the purchase of a suitable vessel."

Swift as a striking serpent, the stranger's lean hand vanished into his cloak and reappeared to spill a handful of glittering stones on the wine-ringed wood between them.

43

Winking up in the ruddy firelight lay a princeling's ransom in sapphires blue as the southern seas, emeralds like cat's eyes glowing in the dark, topazes and zircons as yellow as a Khitan's skin, and rubies as scarlet as fresh-spilt blood.

Conan, unimpressed, fixed the stranger with a suspicious glare. "First," he growled, "I want to know who in Crom's name you are. Curse it, I take no gift from a man who hides his face even here in an Argossean inn, with King Ariostro's guardsmen on every street, making the city so safe a juicy wench can walk the length of the waterfront unmolested!"

With a smile in his purring voice, the stranger replied: "I thank you for the implied compliment, seaman! I hide my face here for good reason, as Argos-folk know my features all too well."

"Well then, your name!" rumbled Conan. "Or I'll pitch you across the room as I did that fat-arsed bully."

"Gladly, to put you at your ease," the other laughed. Drawing himself up a little, he said softly: "Know, sailor, that I am Ariostro, king of Argos!"

Conan grunted with astonishment. The stranger drew off one of his gloves and extended the bare hand. The ancient royal seal ring of the Argossean monarchy blazed in the firelight with the brilliance of the huge diamond in which the royal sigil was cut.

IV. Scarlet Tortage

Black waves break on the wet, black shore
    In a thunder of shattering spray—
But what care we if the storm gods roar,
And lash at the pane and claw at the door,
    And we sail at the break of day?
A lone gull cries like a poor, damned soul
    That the waves have washed away—
But what care we if the cold seas roll?
There's ale in the cup and wine in the bowl,
    And the dawn is hours away!
                    —*Barachan pirate chant*

TORTAGE ROARED defiance to the stars. In a cup of rocky cliffs, the pirate port blazed with light and resounded with roaring song, for the Red Brotherhood was in. Tall caracks and slim caravels bobbed at their moorings along the stone quays and wooden piers or lay at anchor in the harbor. Every alehouse, wine shop, inn, and brothel did a roaring business, when half the freebooters of the Western Sea swaggered through the cobbled alleys of red Tortage with pouches bursting with gold, bellies bulging with beer and ale, and hearts inflamed by lust and truculence.

45

Wine-shop signs, blazoned with skulls, torches, crossed scimitars, dragons, gryphons, crowned heads, and other devices swung creakingly in the stiff sea wind. Surf boomed as it broke at the foot of the cliffs that loomed against the stars above the little town.

Salt spray exploded against the docks, and the whistling wind carried its warm, salt splatter through the crooked streets that wound past low, flat-roofed houses, walled with whitewashed stucco, with iron grilles over their windows. The wind made the fronds of the palm trees lash like fly whisks against the dancing stars above.

For two hundred years and more, the little town in the cliff-walled cove had been the capital of a pirate empire that scourged the seas between Pictland and Kush. Here no law ruled but the rude and simple pact of the Brotherhood. Beyond that, the only law was the fist, the knife, the sword, and the skill of the battler.

Tonight the pirate city was ablaze with roaring mirth and song. Duels over some slight, real or fancied, exploded in the streets. Rings of shouting men gathered about the cursing duellists, who fought to the death over an accidental shove, a trivial insult, or the favors of some red-lipped, hip-swinging wench. This was a night to remember. The ships were in, their holds gorged with treasure—the loot of the merchant fleets of the southern seas. And Amra the Lion had returned!

Thirty years had not yet buried his portentous name in forgetfulness. On the contrary, the passage of time had only added fresh luster to the legends of his swashbuckling days, in the wild times of Bêlit, the Shemitish she-pirate, and Red Ortho, and grim Zaporavo of Zingara. In those distant days, when Vilerus and then Numedides had reigned in Aquilonia, Conan had come among them—first as Bêlit's partner in command of a bloodthirsty crew of black corsairs; then, years later, as a pirate of the Barachas and a leader of Zingaran buccaneers.

For several years off and on, his ships—the galley *Tigress*, the caravel *Red Lion*, and the carack *Wastrel*—had sailed the seas, returning heavy-laden with treasure.

For a time Amra, as some called him, or Conan, as he was known to others, had stood tall among the captains of the Red Brotherhood. But then he had vanished into the little-known lands of the interior and was heard of on the Main no more. Tales and legends spread from these inland realms of a wild, unconquerable warrior-king named Conan, but few of his old seafaring comrades—even those who had known Conan by that name—recognized, in the inland monarch, the Cimmerian pirate of former days. Thus Amra became a myth of the fading past.

But now he stood among them, towering up into the flaring orange light of torches, with the salt sea wind tugging at his gray mane and iron-hued beard. Torchlight winked and sparkled on the coat of chain mail that clothed his massive arms and torso. His great black cloak streamed behind him, billowing like the wings of some gigantic bird of prey.

Conan stood atop a stone bench in the midst of the port city's main square, and his voice rose like a trumpet above the murmur of the throng. It filled their lawless hearts with echoes of splendid deeds and epic battles of long ago and the promise of stupendous enterprises yet to come. For Amra the Lion had swaggered out of the mists of legend to recruit a crew for some unknown venture into the Western Sea. Into that wind-lashed waste of waters, no ship had ventured in the memory of man. Who but Amra would dare to dream of so fantastic an adventure?

They stood gaping as his words intoxicated them, for the wild and lawless magic of his own heroic spirit was as contagious as fire in tinder. Gold and gems he promised them, wealth and glory, and the fame of a great adventure into the Unknown, among new seas, forgotten isles, and strange peoples. They should venture into the deeps of

47

nameless seas, whence they would emerge, not as lawless rogues, but as fabulous adventurers—heroes whose haloes of legend would beguile soft wenches and win immortal fame in songs and epics for aeons to come.

And there at anchor rode Amra's ship—a stout, deep-bellied carack called the *Red Lion*, like Amra's caravel of former times.

Conan did not reveal all the story. He did not tell them of King Ariostro of Argos, whose gems had purchased the mighty vessel. And why frighten them away with tales of the Red Shadows and the weird apparition of Epemitreus, the long-dead prophet?

For, just as the Terror had carried away hundreds of Conan's subjects, so the mysterious curse had struck at the citizens of Argos. Ariostro's court magicians and seers had read the omens of the stars. They had opened certain long-undisturbed books of magical lore and told their king that the Red Shadows struck from some unknown realm beyond the mysterious Western Ocean.

Ship after ship had the shrewd and able king of Argos launched into the Western Sea, but none had ever returned with a clue to the mystery. At length, even his navy grew nervous at the hint of further ventures into the unknown West. But still the Red Shadows struck and slew, and the kingdom hovered on the edge of mutiny and rebellion.

So, venturing into the streets of Messantia in disguise, King Ariostro had searched for reckless master mariners whom he might persuade to undertake the adventure. For this last desperate gamble, he had found the men he sought in Conan the Cimmerian—whose identity he quickly divined, although he was too discreet to betray the fact—and Sigurd Redbeard, the bluff and hearty old sea rover from distant Vanaheim. With his gems, they had bought the powerful carack and were now come into port to enlist a crew of lawless rogues from among the Barachan pirates.

Some of the faces among the throng were known to Conan from his pirate days of old, and to them he spoke out boldly. One gigantic, grinning black from the southern jungles caught his eye. He thrust out an arm toward the majestic Kushite, whose bare arms gleamed like oiled ebony in the orange light of the blown torches, and whose bulbous mass of kinky black hair was streaked with gray.

"You know me, Yasunga!" he thundered. "You were but a lad when I roved the black coast, years and years ago by the side of your bold mistress, Bêlit. What of you? Will you join my venture?"

Yasunga threw up his long, black arms with a shout of joy. "Ya Amra! Amra!" he roared, drunken with old memories.

"Back, you black dog!" snarled a voice in chill, deadly tones, as a slim, deadly form thrust itself in front of the black and pushed him back into the crowd. The man turned to fix Conan with coldly venomous eyes.

Conan looked down at the newcomer with narrowing eyes, taking in the lean, sallow face with inky brows and thin lips, the slim, sinewy body in a breastplate of polished, gold-inlaid steel over black velvet, the diamonds flashing at earlobe and wrist, where a lean, strong hand jutted from amidst foaming lace to fondle the well-worn hilt of a long cut-and-thrust rapier.

In a soft voice, whose lisping accents marked him for a Zingaran, the black-clad, sallow man addressed the crowd: "Back to your kennels, dogs! Do you listen to the wild dreams of this crazy old fool, who has come out of nowhere to lure you with wild promises on a harebrained quest into the unknown? Mayhap this be the same Amra of whose deeds we have heard—and mayhap not. What matters it? Amra or no, this deluded old wolf has come amongst us to disrupt the Brotherhood. What care we for adventures and glory? We are practical men, earning our living from the sea, and to the eleven scarlet Hells with dream-befuddled heroes!"

He glared contemptuously at Conan. "And seek not to lure my navigator, Yasunga, into your mad schemes, gray dog. I taught him the lore of sun and stars—and by Mitra, he stays with me: Black Alvaro, of the *Falcon of Zingara!* So up anchor and take your rotten carack back to whatever port of dreams you hale from. We have no room for your sort here."

Alvaro had half turned to stride away through the muttering throng, when Conan's deep bellow of laughter stiffened him. Conan spat loudly.

"Old gray dog is it, you girl-faced, fancy-clad, soft-gutted whelp of a nameless Kordavan gutter slut? I was a captain of the Coast when you were still puking up your mother's thin, sour milk. I was pouring half the gold of a dozen cities into the alleys of Tortage when you were still fondling boys in the back of a Zingaran whorehouse. If you've no guts for an honest venture, then slink back to your fetid kennel—but there are others here with more manhood in one hand than you have in your yellow-bellied body. I speak to them, not you. And, yes, I'm old— but I still know a trick or two, which I shall be pleased to show you if you like!"

Black Alvaro whirled with a curse, his rapier rasping out and glittering in the glare of the torches like a needle of fire. Whooping, the crowd formed a ring.

Conan tossed aside his bellying black cloak and drew his heavy Aquilonian broadsword. But, even before the blade cleared the scabbard or he could step down from the bench on which he stood, Alvaro lunged with a dancer's grace.

The steel needle flicked out at Conan's unarmored face, but with one booted foot he kicked the lancing blade aside and sprang down from the bench. His sword sang from its worn leather sheath and rang like a bell as it met the Zingaran blade. Steel music clashed in the windy silence as the two combatants circled, advanced, retreated, cut, parried, and thrust. The torches sent their billowing shadows crawling over the walls of the nearer houses.

Men sucked in their breaths, for Alvaro of the *Falcon* was accounted the deadliest blade among the Isles—and Amra, gray with years, was an unknown adversary. They measured his towering bulk and mighty limbs against the lean, silken grace of the Zingaran and cast bets at wildly fluctuating odds.

Alvaro soon found that his singing blade could never quite dodge past Conan's guard. The great broadsword, made for smashing armor, seemed ill-chosen for a fencing match against the lighter blade; it should have been slow and unwieldy. But in Conan's leathery hand it danced as lightly as a willow wand. Nor did the fiercely grinning old Cimmerian seem to tire from the heft of it. His arm seemed as tireless and rigid as an iron bar.

Sweat glistened on Alvaro's brow beneath his flying black ringlets. Sweat beaded his thin lips and trickled down his hollow cheeks. He knew that if blade ever met blade with full impact, his rapier would be shattered into flying fragments.

But Conan was not even trying to bring the full weight of his longsword to bear. Instead, with incredible ease, he wove a glittering wall of flying steel before him, through which the flashing point of the Zingaran's light blade could not gain entry. From time to time, Conan's grin broadened into deep laughter. He was playing with the agile but wearying Zingaran, and the chilling thought went through Alvaro that at any time the Cimmerian could beat his rapier aside and cut him down.

The crowd hung breathlessly on the ringing play of shimmering steel. Gradually they came to sense the same fact. Yasunga, the giant Kushite who had known Amra long before, started a chant, which soon rose from hundreds of throats, until it seemed to the gasping, sweating Alvaro that the square shook with its throbbing thunder:

"*Am-ral Am-ral Am-ral*"

The pulsing cry rose and rose until it boomed like the pounding of the waves. The driving rhythm shook the lithe Zingaran's normally icy nerve. With one hand, Alvaro fumbled behind him, beneath his short mantle of black velvet. There, thrust through his girdle, a slim, wavy-bladed Shemite dagger was thrust for use on such occasions as this. His fingers drew the blade from its slender scabbard and palmed the hilt, so that the wavy blade lay against his forearm.

Then he disengaged and sprang back several paces. He stood panting and disheveled, while Conan's flashing blade slowed to a halt.

"Had enough, black swine of Zingara?" the old wolf growled.

The dirk flashed in the torchlight as it whirled through the dark air toward Conan's bare throat. Without appearance of haste, Conan's left hand reached up and caught the dagger by its hilt, snatching it out of the air as it flew.

This amazing feat brought a roar from the throng. They had heard that the hillmen of fabulous eastern lands played the deadly game of plucking flying knives from the air, but never had they seen it done. None knew of the long years Conan had spent on the bleak steppes of Hyrkania, and amidst the coasts and isles of the Vilayet Sea, and in the towering Himelian Mountains, as nomad chief, pirate on an inland sea, and mercenary warrior. In those years he had mastered the use of the deadly Hyrkanian bow, the keen Zuagir tulwar, the dismembering Zhaibar knife, and other Eastern weaponry.

The shock of the deed glazed Alvaro's eyes with horror. The air seemed to stifle him. He tore open the lace colar above his cuirass and stood uncertainly, as if he knew not what to do next. Tension grew taut as a bowstring.

Then—Conan gave him back his knife. It flashed through the air and sank to the hilt in Alvaro's bare throat. For a moment the Zingaran stood on wavering legs, with his face as pale as a dish of curds and blood trickling down over his gleaming cuirass. Then he fell with a clang to the cobbles.

Conan tossed his great sword up, caught it again, and sheathed it. The crowd went wild with a thunderous cry:

"Am-ral Am-ral Am-ral!"

V. The Black Kraken

The Kraken lives, that anciently arose
  from seething primal slime,
In lands long since submerged by time, beneath
  the gray, endragoned sea.
                    —*The Visions of Epemitreus*

THE *Red Lion* was three days out from the Barachan Isles
when her people sighted the green galley.

It was dawn of the third day. Naked to the waist, with
his heavy broadsword hanging at his side, Conan stood on
the poop deck drinking deep of the clean salt wind. Spray
had stiffened his mane and beard with salt. A sunrise of
golden flame drenched the east with light and set the long,
thin clouds afire. The brisk northeasterly trade wind
sang in the carack's rigging and bellied out the broad sails
above.

"Ho, Amra! Up with the dawn, eh?" boomed a deep
voice. Conan turned to see Sigurd standing spraddle-
legged at the rail, roaring with good humor. The wind ruffled his flaming bush of beard and stung his apple-red
cheeks to an even ruddier hue. It spread the wings of his

54

billowing crimson cloak, which had once adorned the back of a pompous Zingaran admiral.

Conan grinned at the spectacle the bluff old Northman made. The golden thread that covered his cloak with embroidered arabesques was worn and tarnished, and several of the big, ornate ivory buttons were missing. A sash of many clashing colors, which bristled with the usual half-dozen jeweled dirks, bludgeons, and a hugh scimitar with a notched blade, girdled Sigurd's massive belly. Under the vast cloak, the old Vanr wore a patched, torn white blouse, spotted with wine stains and gravy. It was open to the navel, and through the opening bristled the silver-shot red fur that thatched the Northman's chest. A gaudy scarlet kerchief was wound about his bald head, and glittering hoops of gold wobbled from each ear.

"Hah! By Heimdal's horn and Tanit's veil, 'tis a morning for the very gods, eh, Lion?" he said. " 'Tis like wine to me thirsty guts to be at sea again with a good deck under me heels and a crew of rascally cutthroats ready at call to fill the nine seas with blood!"

"Aye," growled Conan. "It is a stout ship the king of Argos' gems got us, and as staunch a crew of rogues as ever I shipped with in the old days."

He peered down into the waist, where the crew scrubbed the deck and performed other sailorly chores. The legends that burned with lurid light around the name of Amra the Lion had brought a full complement of seasoned sea-thieves, eager to share the glory and loot of Amra's venture into the dim West. They were a motley lot, the throng of men that milled and toiled in the waist with half-naked brown bodies, smelling of tar and sour wine, but the very cream of the pirates of the Barachas.

The largest group was composed of Argosseans, men of medium height and sturdy build, with brown or tawny hair. Mixed with these were a number of olive-skinned, black-browed Zingaran renegades. There were men of Ophir and Koth. There were a few swarthy, hook-nosed Shemites with blue-black hair and beards, and even a huge, brown-skinned, hawk-faced Stygian or two. There was a stocky, fair-haired Zaporoskan—Yakov, the bow-master. There was a black giant from jungled Kush, with the sunlight gleaming on his glossy hide—Yasunga, the navigator. There was a powerful, brown-skinned man with a curly black beard—Goram Singh of Vendhya, a land so far to the east and so little known that many Westerners thought it a mere fable. But, white or brown or black, they were veteran seaman all.

Sigurd fixed Conan with a keen blue eye. "Now, what's the plan, mate? Fine words and resounding promises of glittering loot, but what is it we look for in the Western Ocean, and whither are we bound? So far we've seen naught but a few whales."

Conan shrugged. "Crom knows, not I! But I've heard men talk of lost continents and fabulous isles beyond the sunset. And from the hints the shade of Epemitreus let fall, and the counsels of King Ariostro's pack of glib-tongued star-watchers, I gather we just keep on the westward and watch for anything unlikely and odd. Devil take me, Northman, I hope we find the source of the Terror soon! This taste of sea life makes me hungry for a trifle of action. Peace is beautiful, but . . ." Conan eased his broadsword out of its scabbard and cut the air with a swish that could be heard above the sough of the wind.

Redbeard laughed with a deep chuckle that shook his paunch. He cocked a tufted eyebrow at the glowering Cimmerian.

"Ho ho, mate!" he snorted. "So that's the way the wind lies, is it? Ye're still the cunning, black-hearted rascal I knew of old. When we've fought this shadowy foe, as we promised, shall we turn about for a bit of honest roguery? There were fat merchantmen tied up in Messantia's harbor, and 'twould be a fine joke to loot Argos's ships with the very ship their king furnished, would it not?"

Conan smiled a grim, cynical smile and clapped Sigurd on the shoulder. "Same thieving old walrus, you are! No, I like not the taste of that."

"Don't tell me that, after all these years, ye've turned honest!"

Conan uttered a bark of laughter. "Not I! But being a king does spoil a man's taste for the pettier forms of thievery. Besides, Ariostro has never given me trouble, so why should I trouble him? Conn will have enough problems, guarding his frontiers against the neighboring kingdoms, without my stirring them up."

"Then—do ye mean to take a crack at the Stygians, as I was for doing when we met in Messantia? They're a fell and hardy lot; but with this crew we might just—"

Conan shook his head. "Not that, even. After all, I've been a pirate captain, and a bloody successful one, several times over. Why should I climb that same ladder once more?"

"Well, then," growled Sigurd impatiently, "what in all the flaming hells is it ye mean? Out with it, man!"

Conan flung out a long arm, and a gnarled forefinger stabbed toward the bow. "Away to westward, mate, there's something we know naught about. The Red Shadows are part of it. There are hints in old manuscripts that may be a part of it, too." A deep laugh rumbled in Conan's chest. "You can't imagine me as a scholar, now can you?"

"It were easier to think of one of Ariostro's pretty little dancing girls as a bloody-handed pirate."

"Well, I can read a few different scripts. And in the royal library at Tarantia I found tales of the Cataclysm, when the ocean gulped down Atlantis, eight thousand years ago. They tell, these tales, how thousands of Atlanteans fled to the Mainland—or Thuria, as they used to call it. And in the iron-bound Book of Skelos it said:

'Others fled from sinking Atlantis to westward, and it is said that thither they came upon another continent, over against the Thurian continent and bounding the Western Ocean on the farther side. But what befell these refugees I know not, for with the destruction of Atlantis the trackless ocean became too wide for the ships of those days to maintain a regular commerce betwixt the lands we know and the unknown western land.' That is all, but it may very well be connected with our present mission."

"Well?" said Sigurd. "I've heard tales like that, too."

"Well, if there be a land of mighty sorcery ahead of us, it will also be a land of wealth and power, ripe for enterprising rascals like us to pluck. Why fool around with the loot of a few ships when, with some luck and some guts, we can take an empire?"

Sigurd sighed and wiped his eyes with the backs of his hairy hands. "Ah, Amra, I might have knowed ye'd have some scheme in your thick skull, madder and wilder than anything any ordinary man could think up! 'Tis a fine old wolf ye are, my word upon it! Though they feed us to dragons when we get there, I'll ship with you as far as the sunset itself, by all the gods!"

He broke off to peer suspiciously at the sun. With a snort of anger, he waddled to the nearer of the quarter rudders, where a one-eyed Shemitish ruffian stood to the watch.

"Avast, ye hooknosed dog! Be ye blind or stinking drunk?" he roared, cuffing the startled seaman aside and seizing the tiller in capable paws. "We're riding half a point off the course ye set last night, Amra! Curse and rot these lazy pigs—the scum of the Barachas, by the bowels of Ahriman and the breasts of Ishtar!" He squinted ferociously at the sun and thrust the tiller over with a practiced heave. The *Red Lion* heeled slightly, responding like a well-trained steed.

Then a cry came ringing down from above. "Sail ho!"

Conan sprang to the rail and raked the gray, misty seas with keen eyes. But he could see nothing.

"Whither away?" he boomed through cupped hands. The reply floated down from the lookout at the foretop: "Point and a half off the port bow!"

"I see her!" The old Northman was again at Conan's side, puffing like an asthmatic walrus, having shoved the one-eyed sailor back to the tiller. "There she be—and by all the gods, she looks like a galley!"

Conan shaded his eyes with one hand and followed Sigurd's pointing finger. There, looming out of the coiling morning haze, were two slender, bare masts. When the *Red Lion* rose on the long swell, those on her poop deck could glimpse the long, low hull of a galley beneath this rigging.

"Now what in the scarlet Hells of the Stygian Set-worshipers," rumbled Conan, "is a galley doing out here? We must be fairly close to land. No skipper with all his wits would sail far out into the Western Ocean in such a craft. If the long swells didn't swamp her, the crew would collapse from lack of food and water and from not having a place to lie down."

The galley was now closer, so that they could see the sleek lines of her low, sea-green hull. White foam flashed along her sides, and Conan saw the twinkle of sunlight on dripping water from her double bank of oars—a bireme, with a high, curved prow carved of brass into the likeness of a dragon's head. Below this figurehead, level with the waterline, a long, viciously pointed bronze ram, green with verdigris and spotted with barnacles, cut through the waves.

"Hm, that's cursed odd, Amra!" grumbled Sigurd. "She flies no banner. Well, you said we were to look for oddities."

Conan shrugged. "What's that painted on her bow?"

Sigurd peered. "Looks like a black cloud with a red center, or is it a black starfish?"

Conan glowered on the strange green galley. "Well, she's no merchantman but a war galley, with that ram in her stem and double banks of oars. Let's let her pass; she'd give us hard knocks and no loot . . ."

Still, he thought, it was strange to find such a ship hovering about these untraveled waters. Could it be that which they sought? Throwing back his gray mane, Conan called out to the watchman on the foretop.

"Ahoy there! Can you make out the marking on her prow?"

"Aye, Captain. 'Tis a black thing like a devilfish, with a fringe of tentacles around a burning eye—"

Conan's voice rose in a mighty bellow: "Helmsman! Two points to port; head straight for that galley. All hands on deck! Swords, pikes, and defenses! Stand by to trim sail. Archers, to the forecastle deck, with your gear! Yasunga, make up a boarding party. Hop to it, swabs! Here's the fight you've been spoiling for."

Sigurd peered at him, baffled. "What in the name of Mitra?"

"The sign of the Black Kraken, you red dog of Vanaheim! Does that mean naught to you? Stir your befuddled wits!" growled Conan.

Sigurd followed Conan about the poop and halted when the Cimmerian did to let the cabin boy lace him into his coat of mail and settle the horned helmet on his head. The Northman's brow was knotted in thought. Then his frown relaxed, but his face paled.

"Do ye mean," he said slowly, "that old tale about the emblem of the Witch Kings of Atlantis?"

"I do. Now get your cuirass on, before they spill those fat guts of yours all over the deck."

"Gods of the sea!" said Sigurd, turning slowly away.

"The Kraken of the Atlanteans, that should all have been decently drowned eight thousand years agone . . . Crom, Badb, and Ishtar! Can it be?"

Although she was clearly no merchantman bearing loot, the green galley turned and fled before the *Red Lion* on the morning wind. On each of her two masts, a high-peaked, triangular sail bloomed and filled with the following breeze. The *Red Lion* followed close upon her foaming track.

Conan had clambered into the rigging and clung with one bronzed hand while the other shaded his eyes.

"Odd—cursed odd!" he muttered. "All oars in motion, yet I'm damned for a Stygian if I can see a single oarsman on the benches. She seems bare of fighting men as well; none on her poop or forecastle deck, and not a hand aloft in her rigging."

He lowered himself to the deck, where Sigurd and the giant black, Yasunga, stood.

"Cursed odd indeed, Amra," said the old Northerner. "And look at the cut of her hull! I've never seen such a ship in all me days."

"Green ship of Hell," muttered Yasunga in his deep, musical bass. "Ship of ghosts, Amra!"

"Belay that!" barked Conan. "Ship of Hell or ship of earth, she's running free as if she bore the Empress of Khitai and all her treasure! Look at that stem slice the swells!" He raised his voice. "Milo! Hoist the raffee tops'l! And if you get the lines fouled I'll skin you." He spoke to Sigurd and Yasunga again: "She's fast, with both oars and sails; but with our greater spread of sail we may run her down yet. Wherever she's from, she's in a hurry to shake us off her tail!"

"But with no escort," growled Sigurd. "Damned suspicious! Whoever heard of a king's galley or treasure ship barging around the seas without extra protection?"

The crew had now mustered in their places. Archers were stringing their bows on the forecastle deck and looking over the arrows in their quivers to make sure that none had warped. In the waist, men stood to the ropes, while the deck fighters clustered at the rail, buckling the chin straps of helmets, tying the laces of cuirasses and leather jacks, and sharpening their cutlasses with whetstones.

"By Crom!" boomed Conan. "We'll find out what she bears so precious that she flees like a frightened maid at the mere sight of us!"

The men, inflamed by the excitement of the chase, sent up a cheer. Sigurd, now covered from neck to crotch by a shirt of bronzen scales sewn to leather, puffed up the ladder to the poop deck. Conan clapped him on the shoulder.

"Crom and Mitra, old sea horse, but the taste of battle makes my heart swell like that of an old charger sniffing blood!"

The Northman grinned broadly and gave a bellow of joy that would have summoned a hippogriff in the mating season had one been within earshot.

"Hah! Well, Lion, old Sigurd said things would look up soon, and here they are! I have a feeling in me bones that this'll be a treasure the likes of which we never saw in all our days."

"Aye?" laughed Conan. "Then let's at it!"

With every sail she possessed filled with wind, the carack plunged after her prey. The following swells boosted her along, slowly rising and falling as they foamed by underneath her. Her blunt bow threw up twin fans of green foam, and white foam bubbled in her wake. And ever ahead of her, pitching on the swells, the mysterious green galley rowed and sailed, her two triangular sails set wing-and-wing, like the leathery pinions of some flying reptile of old.

VI. Magic Fire

A long, green galley from the unknown West,
The dread Black Kraken on her bow impressed,
In full sail hastens from a land untold,
With Hell's foul secret in her deep, dark hold.
                              —*The Voyage of Amra*

The sun hung high in the clear, blue vault when the
Red Lion at last caught up with the mysterious green
galley with the symbol of the Black Kraken of Atlantis on
her bow. All morning the galley fled before them, with her
tall black triangular sails swollen with the wind and her
oars rising and falling as if her oarsmen knew no human
fatigue. But, foot by foot, the big carack closed the distance
between them.

Conan, in a horned steel helmet and a long shirt of link
mail over a haqueton of soft leather, strode about the deck,
inspecting the arms and armor of his boarding party. Then
he climbed back to the poop, where Sigurd stood spraddle-
legged, watching the galley's every move and barking commands to the steersmen who stood with muscular, brown
arms gripping the twin tillers.

"She's giving up the chase at last and putting about," grunted Sigurd.

As if owning the futility of flight, the galley was turning and slowing as the *Red Lion* neared. Now they were almost within bowshot. Conan glanced to the forecastle deck, where Yakov's archers stood behind the wicker mantlets hung along the rail, awaiting the command to shoot.

"Strange, Amra," grumbled the Northman. "Still no one on deck!"

"It is cursed strange," agreed Conan. "They should at least have a party gathered to repel boarders. Are they all hiding below like mice, or is there nobody aboard but the oarsmen and steersmen?"

"We're getting close," said Sigurd.

Facing the bow where the archers stood, Conan raised his voice to a bellow: "Shoot one!"

"Aye, aye, Captain," Yakov called back. The bowmaster tapped an archer on the shoulder. The man drew his bow to the ear and released with a flat twang. The arrow arched over the intervening gulf of water, to fall ten paces short. For a short while the crew stood silent as the wind sighed, the water hissed, and the ships wallowed.

"Shoot one!"

This time the shaft thudded home in the enameled planking.

"In range!" boomed Sigurd.

"One volley, your command!" roared Conan.

"Aye, aye!" Yakov lined up his archers. Presently all the bows released at once. With a swish like the rush of wings, a flight of arrows swept across the narrowing gulf and thudded home, mostly out of sight behind the mantlets that lined the rail of the galley.

Conan narrowly watched the action of the galley's oars. Ordinarily, such a volley of arrows should have struck at least a few of the rowers, disorganizing the beat of the oars until the men hit could be replaced or their oars shipped.

But the oars of the galley, in two banks, continued to rise and fall at the same unvarying, mechanical beat.

"She must be full-decked," grunted Conan.

"I think she's turning to ram us," said Sigurd.

"Right. Keep our head toward her. If we hit her bow on, we'll drive her down and break her ram."

The Vanr bellowed commands to the steersmen and to the sailors at the lines. The tillers were put up and the sails trimmed to take the wind abeam as the *Red Lion* swung to port to keep the galley dead ahead. Unseen hands brailed the galley's sails up against their yards.

The galley continued her swing, and for an instant the two ships rushed at each other head-on. From the poop, Conan got a good view of the galley's deck. Not a soul was to be seen.

Then the galley, as if losing courage at the sight of the tall, massive bow of the *Red Lion* foaming down upon her, turned again to port, heeling with the sharpness of her turn. A mere fifty paces away, Conan could plainly discern the strange black emblem blazoned on the bow. More like a circular cloud of dense, black vapor it seemed, with whorls of mist escaping in tentacular wisps, than a literal devilfish. But the crimson eye, glaring from the center of the black mass, blazed with lust and fury.

Still nobody was to be seen on deck. The green galley could have been a ghost ship, bare of mortal life.

"No watch in the rigging! Not a hand on deck! Not even a helmsman at the tiller!" rumbled Sigurd uneasily. "By Badb and Mitra, I like it not, mate, not a bit of it!"

"Yakov!" called Conan. "Have your lads shoot through the oar holes!"

Bowstrings snapped and arrows hissed. Many struck the wood alongside the oar slots, but many more—at that short range—whipped out of sight through the holes and vanished. But there were none of the expected yells of pain and clatter of oars striking one another that would normally be expected. A second volley produced no different result. Now the galley was running free again, and her triangular sails stood out to take the wind. The *Red Lion* swung downwind to follow.

"Fire arrows, Yakov!" roared Conan. "By Crom, I'll rouse some life in that black-sailed bastard yet."

There were a few moments of frantic activity on the forecastle deck as torches were fetched from the galley and rags were dipped in oil and wound about the shafts of arrows. Presently a shower of flaming arrows, trailing tails of black smoke, whistled into the mantlets and thudded into the bare, green decks. In an instant, plumes of dirty black smoke crawled up from a dozen spots about the ship, to be whipped away by the brisk breeze.

"Ha!" thundered Conan. "That did it! Look, Sigurd!"

On the green galley's ornate poop deck now stood a tall, gaunt figure. This, from his appearance, was no ordinary seaman. His bony form was wrapped in many-pleated cotton garments, while a fantastic cloak of gorgeous green feathers was thrown over his narrow shoulders. His sallow, swarthy pate was shaven; his stern, gaunt features might have been cast in brass for all their mobility. Looking more like a priest or a wizard than a seaman, he stood motionless on the gaudily decorated afterdeck, watching the *Red Lion* with a venomous glare in his sharp, black eyes.

As Conan and his crew watched, the man suddenly extended a bony arm in a curious gesture. As he did so, each fire smouldering on the deck went abruptly out. The spirals of smoke faded and vanished.

"Magic!" boomed Sigurd wrathfully, clutching Conan's shoulder with a grip like a steel trap.

"Yakov!" yelled Conan. "Feather that dog!"

But before the order could be carried out, the tall, feather-robed figure plucked a small flask from under his robe

66

and cast it over the side, to splash in the surging green waters between the two ships.

As the flask struck the waves, the heaving water erupted into an explosion of dazzling flame. A wall of seething, crimson fire sprang up between the two ships. Conan's men shouted with astonishment, gesticulating with wonder. Consternation and superstitious fear was written on their features. They were brave enough to face sharp steel and whistling shafts for the chance of loot and rapine—but who could fight sorcery?

"Magic!" Sigurd repeated. "By the heart of Ahriman and the loins of Tammuz, do ye see it, Amra? Yonder slant-eyed wizard builds a wall of fire in less time than it takes a man to spit!"

Staring with narrowed eyes, Conan noted that the unnatural flames did not spread, as they should have if caused by some inflammable oil. They remained in one position, forming a wall of flame that almost hid the alien galley and that leaped so high as to threaten the *Red Lion*'s mainsail.

"Eight points to port! Trim sail for wind on the port beam!" bellowed Conan. "We'll see if we can go around it," he added to Sigurd.

"By the guts of Shaitan and Ymir's beard, the fire *follows* us!" said Sigurd, clutching the rail with whitened knuckles.

And so it was. As the *Red Lion* swung upwind to port, the wall of fire moved as if to keep itself between the carack and the fleeing galley. Conan shaded his eyes to look at his imperiled canvas overhead. As yet it had not caught fire—in fact, did not even look singed. Nor did the thick, oily smoke so much as smudge the white sails. Conan burst into laughter.

"Steersmen ho!" he thundered. "Tillers down, and pay no mind to the fire! Trim sail to run free!"

"Amra?" said Sigurd, goggling. "What in the name of all the devils—"

Conan grinned through his bristling gray beard. "Watch, old walrus, and learn."

The *Red Lion* clove through the burning wall as if it were not there. The ship's company felt no heat of its passage. Once on the other side, the magical barrier winked out of existence. The crew gaped with astonishment.

"Just a mirage, and illusion!" roared Conan. "Now muster for boarding, dogs, and we'll see how yon feather-robed sorcerer likes cold steel!"

As the bow of the *Red Lion* came closer and closer to the stern of the galley, those on the carack could see the stern, masklike features of the shaven-skulled magician working with rage. Then he lifted both arms, so that his gorgeous cloak spread in the wind like the blazing pinions of some legendary phoenix.

"*Hai, Xotlil Chahuatepak ya-xingothl*" he screamed.

And the Red Shadows struck. From the four quarters of the sky they gathered, as they had on that deadly day when they first appeared in Conan's royal palace. They clung about a screaming Argossean helmsman, and he winked out of existence. The *Red Lion* lurched as the man at the other tiller strove to keep her on course by his unaided strength.

This was no illusion. As Conan watched, the feathered sorcerer laughed an ugly cackle, and spread his arms to summon the Terror again.

This time, his eyes were full upon Conan.

VII. The Phantom Warriors

Though manned by devils and walled with flame
From pits infernal, whence she came,
The Lion will break the galley's spell
And rape the treasure shipped from Hell!
                              —*The Voyage of Amra*

OLD SIGURD saw, understood, and quick-wittedly roared a command to Yakov on the forecastle deck: "Skewer that devil in the feathers!"

Bowstrings twanged, and swift shafts flashed over the green water toward the high, gilded poop where the magician stood, arms raised to summon the Terror again. As the arrows hissed toward him, he broke off his shadow-conjuring stance to gesture with the flat of his hand. The first shaft was somehow deflected from its target and thudded harmlessly into the deck. The second and third were likewise sent awry—but then several whistled at him at once, too many for him to ward off by his magical powers. And one sank to the feathering in his right hand.

His swarthy features pale with shock, the sorcerer staggered back, nursing his injured hand to his bony chest. He swept the Barachans with a burning glance and vanished.

The pirates recoiled. Sigurd grunted and rubbed his stubby nose. "What can we do against this cursed deviltry, Amra? Shall we turn tail before the Shadows scoop us all up?"

Conan glared. "Have you lost your wits, old walrus? This hell-ship is what we are looking for! 'Tis here the Red Shadows are spawned!"

"But cold steel is no defense against that kind of magic—"

"You saw Yakov's lad put an arrow through the hand of the head devil, didn't you?" growled Conan, cuffing Sigurd on the shoulder. "He'll summon no more devils with that crippled hand, so now's the time to strike!" He strode to the forward end of the poop deck. "Helmsmen, one point to port! Grapnels out! Stand by for collision! Prepare to board!"

The bow of the *Red Lion* slid up parallel with the stern of the galley, and then the massive stem of the carack crunched into the emerald flank of the galley, with a great snapping and shattering of broken oars. Grapnels soared through the air to catch in the alien ship's woodwork, and brawny arms hauled taut the ropes that trailed from them. Other sailors caught the galley's rail with boat hooks.

"Boarders away!" shouted Conan, leaping down the ladder to join the throng of armed men pouring over the rails of the two interlocked ships to the galley's deck, knives in teeth and swords, pikes, and axes in fists. Most of them wore a cuirass of some sort—here a shirt of rusty chain mail; there a leather jack sewn with brass plates or bronze rings. A few of the wilder spirits went naked to the waist. Helmets of a score of designs capped their touseled heads.

Conan's boots crashed through one of the thin wicker mantlets, and he fell heavily into one of the rowing spaces between the deck and the rail. The rowing benches, each wide enough for two men handling a single oar apiece, were sunken half a man's height below the narrow deck. If the benches had been occupied, the heads of the rowers would have risen just above the deck level. But now the benches were empty. Whatever hands had wielded the oars were gone; the oars trailed idly in their oarlocks.

His scalp bristling with the superstitious fears of the barbarian—which all his years in civilization had not wholly ousted—Conan scrambled up out of the rowing space to the main deck. As he did so, glaring about for some foe to fight, the giant black, Yasunga, clutched his arm and pointed to the ornate poop deck.

"Amra, look! The plumed devil!"

The skull-faced wizard had reappeared. Now, instead of his magnificent cloak of feathers, he wore a long coat of chain mail, made from some unknown, rosy metal that blazed in the sunlight. A fantastic helm, shaped like a bird's head, was upon his head. In his left hand he bore a long, straight sword with saw teeth of glittering crystal, such as Conan had never seen in all his wanderings. Strapped to his right arm was a jagged-edged shield of green-enameled metal, embossed with a Kraken emblem like that on the galley's bow.

Conan turned to confront the sorcerer. As he did so, the other uttered a sentence in the same unknown tongue he had spoken in summoning the Red Shadows. A gasp burst from the pirates as astonishment froze them in their tracks.

Where one armed sorcerer had stood, there now stood dozens, all identical to the last detail of dress and features.

"Charge them!" roared Conan, springing up the ladder to the gold-scrolled poop deck and whirling his mighty broadsword. His blade met the swords and shields of the magical army with a metallic crash; Conan was obscurely relieved to find his foes flesh-and-blood men. Tall, gaunt, and lean-muscled, they fought well. But Conan raged like

71

a rabid wolf among them, battering their weapons aside and crunching through their defenses. Behind him, the screaming horde of pirates swarmed up and fell to, so that steel clanged on steel like the beating of anvils in some infernal smithy.

Howling Cimmerian curses, Conan hacked and thrust at the eagle-nosed, cold-eyed faces that rose before him and then fell, slashed and crimsoned. One staggered back from a backhand slash with half his face shorn away. Another fell, clutching at his spilling intestines. A third stumbled back, pawing at the stump of an arm. A fourth fell with bird-helm and skull cloven to the teeth. Still they came on, and still Conan battled with the blind ferocity of the savage he remained at heart.

Eight or nine he must have slain, and now he found himself ringed about by hawk-faced warriors in bird-helms. His blade was notched like a saw and soaked in blood to the hilt. His mail sagged from a dozen rents where the saw-toothed blades had torn it, and his gaunt but mighty shoulders bled from several small, superficial cuts.

Wielding his sword in both hands, he struck at the ring of steel around him, snarling like a trapped wolf. A tenth warrior fell, thrust through the body. Conan knocked several threatening blades aside with a twist of his wrists, feeling the breath sear his lungs and hearing his heart pound like a Pictish war drum. Blood roared in his temples, and he tottered on unsteady legs, but still deadly steel flickered in his hands like lightning and men fell before him.

Now the vision was dimming before his eyes, and the grim ranks of the inexhaustible foe swam in a ruddy mist, and Conan felt the full weight of his sixty-odd years. With half a heart he cursed the gods and fate that he no longer had the iron endurance of his stalwart youth; with the other half, he thanked those same gods that he should fall as he had always wished, face to face with a foe and with steel in hand.

Then, somehow, he had crashed through the hostile ring and confronted a single warrior, who stood at the rear of the deck against the backdrop of sea and sky. In an instant, Conan was upon him. The long blade crunched through the mail links of rosy metal to the foeman's heart —and it was all over.

Gasping and staggering, the Cimmerian whirled to face the rest of the enemy, to find only an empty deck, whereon his own men stood staring. The phantom army had vanished. Every hawknosed warrior had puffed out of existence; even the bodies of the fallen were gone. Conan reeled against the rail. One body remained—that of the last man he had slain. The old Cimmerian hobbled over and, on sudden suspicion, tore away the man's shield. The right hand of the corpse was swathed in bandages.

Conan drew several deep breaths. Then his thunderous laughter stilled the bewildered babble of his pirates.

"They were copies of this dog here," he said, slapping the remaining corpse with the flat of his blade. "They were real, all right—but only so long as he was here to animate them. When he died, they went poof! Now take the wounded back to our own deck. Goram Singh, make up a party to search the forecastle. Hurry up; she's leaking and will soon be awash. If there's any treasure aboard, we had better get it quickly. Sigurd, Yasunga, come with me!"

Conan stumbled down the ladder and thrust open the door of the cabin beneath the poop deck. There, he thought, the sorcerer-captain would probably have berthed. He was bone-weary from the fury of battle and more shaken and exhausted than he wished his men to see. His sixty-odd years weighed down his limbs like armor of lead, and a reviving draught of strong wine would put new strength into his old heart.

Within the shadowy cabin, all was mystic gloom. The walls were hung with strange purple tapestries, whereon

73

horrible demon faces leered and grimaced. On a low taboret of strange design stood a crystal carafe filled with a dark liquid. Conan stumbled across the cabin to drain the contents.

It tasted like wine, but a stronger wine than the Cimmerian had ever encountered. Conan felt its warmth spread through him and put new life into his aching muscles. And then the blood froze within him, for there, hovering near the silken curtains, was the man he had just slain!

It was the same man, for the rosy-hued chain mail was cloven over his heart where Conan had sent the fatal thrust, and blood rilled down from the gash. Paying no heed to the frozen Cimmerian, the spectral figure plucked aside the tapestries, revealing a hidden niche in which was set a silver casket. As Conan watched, the translucent figure of the sorcerer picked up the casket and stepped to the diamond-paned window on the after side of the cabin. The window opened, revealing the foaming blue sea and part of the hull of the *Red Lion.* The phantom was about to step out into the rushing waves, when Conan crashed across the cabin, clutching at the smoky figure and the mysterious chest he sought to bear with him into the deep, blue sea.

"What are you doing, Amra?" cried Sigurd behind him. The Vanr and the Kushite had just crowded into the cabin behind Conan.

Conan's bloody arm encircled the sorcerer's waist but passed through the lean body as easily as if it were made of mist. But the Cimmerian's clutching hand fastened upon a corner of the silver chest. This, at least, was solid, and Conan dragged it out of the feeble clutch of the specter. The ghostly sorcerer toppled out the window, and as he fell he turned upon Conan one ghastly glare of maniacal rage. Then the phantom vanished into the waves.

Conan swayed in the open window, clutching the box and striving to gather his wits to answer the questions that Sigurd and Yasunga showered upon him. To them, the wraith of the sorcerer had not been visible. They had seen the chest rise from its alcove and dart for the window, apparently without support, and they had seen Conan bound after it and seize it.

Before he could satisfy their yammerings, there was a rush of feet outside the cabin and Goram Singh bellowed: "Captain! The forecastle and the hold are empty—not a trace of loot—and the ship is foundering. The deck is awash! We must get back to the *Red Lion!*"

Conan stared down at the small silver casket. This was the green galley's only loot. This was the prize that the magical ship had fled from pirates to keep. This was what the alien sorcerer had fought and died to guard . . .

VIII. The Casket from Atlantis

Where slain suns sink in crimson gore, amidst
   the gloom of brooding skies,
Dim isles of ancient legend rise, where cold
   seas lash the somber shore.
             —*The Visions of Epemitreus*

WITH THE silver box clasped under one arm, Conan vaulted across the rails of the coupled ships, his sheathed broadsword clattering after him. With him came Sigurd and the brawny Vendhyan, Goram Singh. His men were prying grapnels loose from the galley's woodwork and coiling the ropes that trailed from them.

"Cast off!" roared Conan. "Yare! Back the mains'l! Brace the fores'l to starboard—all the way round!"

With a grinding of timbers, the two ships drew apart. Soon a javelin-cast of green, heaving water separated the two. The galley, which had filled from the damage she had received, had settled until her deck was awash and every wave broke and foamed over her. Only her masts and her raised poop and forecastle decks remained consistently above water, on which bits of wreckage danced. Having no dense, heavy cargo to drag her down, she might float thus submerged for months—a menace to other ships, if there were any in these waters—until she drifted ashore or broke up.

"Forward on the main!" commanded Conan. "Furl tops'l and mizzen! Trim sail to run free! Two points to starboard of the wind!"

With a brisk wind filling the mainsail and foresail of the *Red Lion*, the carack responded like a mettlesome steed to the tillers. Away she plunged, over the trackless waves, leaving the wreck of the galley behind her.

At Conan's shoulder, Sigurd watched astern as the wreck sank out of sight. The hearty old Northman was pale and constrained, as were they all. Something about that graceful green hull had struck a note of supernatural terror, like an icy wind from some open tomb. Yasunga shuddered and muttered prayers in his Kushite dialect. Sigurd furtively signed himself, drawing upon his heart with his thumbnail the sign of Thor's hammer.

Soon, even the slender masts of the galley were no longer visible. The sky was clear—blue overhead, rose-red in the west, where a blood-red sun sank slowly into an ominous, inky mass of black vapors. Conan shivered, then clapped Sigurd on the shoulder, rousing the latter from his trance.

"Come to the cabin, Redbeard, where we can toast the fight. And we still have to examine the loot. Yasunga, take the deck!"

Within the cabin, a fire crackled on the hearth and hot water steamed. Conan splashed his naked torso, scrubbed away the dried blood and sweat of battle, and winced at the sting of his scratches and cuts. Then he dried himself with a hot towel, donned a fleecy robe, eased off his boots with a brunt of relief, and sprawled at the table by Sigurd, with his feet in a bucket of hot water. The Northman pushed a flagon of wine toward him. He drank heartily. As he basked in the heat of the fire and felt the inward warmth of the wine, he relaxed into a cheerful good humor.

"Pour me another," he said. "This foray has at least served to blood the men. But there was no real loot, aside from this damned silver box!"

He laid it on the table between them and ran a finger thoughtfully along it. The box was shaped like a brick and not much bigger than one. It was wrought in silver—or was it silver? In the fire's uneven, ruddy glow, the metal glistened with a reddish hue, and to the touch it somehow lacked that cool, oily smoothness of silver.

Sigurd also puzzled over it, running his hairy hand across the raised lines of cryptic pictographs with which the casket was embossed. Then he opened his mouth to speak a word, just as Conan spoke the same word:

"*Orichalcum!*"

The legendary magical metal of lost Atlantis was said to be silver-like in density and weight but with a coppery tinge. Could this casket be a relic of the lost continent? All his days, Conan had relished tales of the old hero-kings of the Atlantean age—mighty Kull of Valusia, lord of the Purple Throne—the terrible Kaa-Yazoth and his Iron Legions—the White Emperor who had been driven from the City of the Golden Gates by the enmity of the black magicians, who had put the sorcerer-king Thevatata on the throne—such tales and sagas, intoned around the tribal fires in his old homeland, had whiled away the long, grim Cimmerian winter nights and planted the seeds of a yearning for travel and adventure that had led him half-way across the world. He stroked the strange box with gentle hands, his eyes softening in a vague dream of bygone glories.

Sigurd, with less room in his mercenary soul for romance, shook the chest. "What do ye suppose is in it?"

"Something precious, by Crom!" laughed Conan.

"That's all the galley held, and that's what it fled to keep from us. Let's crack it open."

There was a keyhole, plainly visible, but the key was doubtless drowned in the smaragdine depths of the unknown sea. Still, a lid has hinges, and hinges can be forced. Conan rummaged in his sea chest. Then he placed the box on end and put the point of a big, bronze needle against the end of the linchpin of the upper hinge. He hammered gently on the needle with the leaden ball that formed the pommel of a massive dirk. He grinned at Sigurd.

"I learned this trick when I was a thief in Zamora—let's see—by Mitra, it's over forty years ago! But I haven't had occasion to use it since."

Soon both linchpins had been forced out of their hinges, and the box lay open. Within lay a small scroll, tied up by a pair of ribbons of scarlet cloth.

"Treasure?" groaned Sigurd. "By the horns of Shaitan and the belly of Moloch! Were ever two honest rogues so put upon? Board a vile galley with bloodshed and battling in the very teeth of half the imps of Hell, and for what? A damned piece of paper!"

He spat expressively. But Conan examined the scroll, grunting: "Don't give up too soon, Redbeard! This is more than a scrap of paper. Aye, Crom blast me if I'm wrong, but it may be as precious as that devil-faced sorcerer thought! Look here."

Sigurd bent to examine the scroll, which Conan had untied and spread out on the table. For one thing, it was not papyrus but some stiff, crackling parchment that might have been made from the tanned hide of flying dragons, such as—the sagas said—the ancient Atlanteans had used. For another, it was obviously a chart, mapping seas that stretched halfway across an unknown world to the west.

"This line here to the east is curved very like the coastline of our own continent," said Conan thoughtfully.

"See? Here's Messantia harbor, and the bulge that curves east from Zingara to Shem . . ."

"Aye, man, and these irregular spots be the Barachas, by Lir and Mannanan!" Sigurd muttered, his brow furrowed. "But gods, look at the expanse of sea to the west!" His stubby forefinger swept westward across the chart from the lines that depicted the coasts with which he was familiar.

"Look there!" said Conan, indicating the coast of an unknown continent along the westward edge of the chart and the chain of seven large islands that lay to the southeast of this land. Although the geography was strange to Conan, the chart had been drawn with a meticulous care for detail in those parts. It showed coasts, harbors, reefs, shoals, and directions of wind and current, proving the cartographer to have been well acquainted with the lands and seas of that region. Conan thumped the table with his fist.

"Crom! I see it now. Do you grasp the secret, Redbeard?"

Sigurd shrugged. Conan tapped the parchment with a long, gnarled finger. "The green ship came from the isles, here, all the way to our coast. Crom knows why, unless 'twas to loose the Red Shadows upon our cities, for some reason we cannot even guess as yet. But what would be so precious to this ship that it would flee our carack like the plague? A chart showing the way home!"

Sigurd blinked. "I think ye've struck the truth, Amra. But then, what are these damned isles?"

"Antillia!"

Sigurd grunted and rubbed a hairy paw over his jowls. "Well, fry me guts, I've heard the tale ere now but never quite believed it. D'ye mean the story that, when Atlantis sank beneath the briny, a band of wizard-priests fled to unknown lands to the west and built there a successor to the Golden Empire? I've heard tell of the walls of the

Seven Cities of the Antilles made of bricks of gold, and streets paved with silver, and temple pyramids of orichalcum, with gems big enough to choke a whale lying on the beaches to be picked up . . . gods and devils, d'ye suppose there's truth in it?"

Conan shrugged. "Crom knows. I heard stories like that about Vendhya and Khitai, but when I went to those places I found that the tales had grown in the telling. The only way to find out is to sail there, and this chart shows our way!"

IX. Voyage on an Unknown Sea

Our sails are full and straining tight,
  Our prow is riding high;
We're out in search of gold tonight
  Beneath a starlit sky.
  —*Sea-Chanty of the Baracha Isles*

AND so it came to pass that the *Red Lion* set forth into
the storm-tossed, monster-haunted wastes of the Western
Ocean, on the strangest of quests. The only guideposts to
show her people the way were the sun by day and the stars
by night, for the compass was unknown to the mariners of
the Hyborian Age, between the foundering of Atlantis
and the rise of Sumeria and Egypt. But, with the chart
from the casket of orichalcum as their guide, they sailed
deeper and deeper into the unknown.

Some balked at this fantastic venture, until Conan
pointed out two good reasons for their consenting to this
quest: first, that they sailed for adventure, glory, and loot,
and would doubtless find all three in plenty in the Seven
Isles of Antillia, amidst the age-old ruins of the last Atlantean cities; second, that he would personally pitch any
grumblers over the side for the krakens to devour. Reasoning of this kind proved remarkably persuasive.

Still, the farther they got from the coasts they knew, the greater grew their superstitious terrors. They remembered old tales, wherein the world was said to end just beyond the horizon. There, the earth fell away in a mighty cliff, over which the oceans poured in an endless flood, down and down to thunder at last against the very foundations of Eternity. According to the tales, any ship that sailed beyond the visible horizon would soon find itself caught in an irresistible current, which would soon carry its helpless, screaming crew right over the world's edge.

Conan squelched this by cracking a few heads together and by pointing out, with unassailable logic, that, with every league west they sailed, the horizon visibly retreated to a corresponding distance.

They sailed on, with full sails straining in the steady blast of the northeast trades. Ahead lay an unknown world; all about was a mysterious waste of wind-torn waves, wherein might lurk fearful denizens of the deep. Conan had little fear of sea monsters. He had faced warriors, wizards, monsters, demons, and even gods. All had proved vulnerable to sharp steel in the final test. But, just to be on the safe side, he had the ship's carpenter rig a catapult and mold some gummy spheres of black tar into whose center he poured lamp oil, with pitchy wicks of old cloth.

As day followed day across the endless waste of waters, Conan came almost to long for some desperate action to break the eternal monotony. But alas, if sea monsters there were, they gave the *Red Lion* a wide berth. To keep his shipload of bloody-handed rogues from getting restless with the inactivity, he kept them busy swabbing the decks, fletching new arrows to replace those expended in the brief battle with the green galley, and toiling at a multitude of other make-work tasks. As an old Hyborian saying had it, *Nergal finds work for idle hands.*

From time to time, the old Cimmerian found himself

83

wondering what was happening in far-off Aquilonia. He thought of his stalwart son and wondered how the young buck liked the weight of a crown on his pate. He thought of his old friends at court, what few of them still lived.

Conan thought, too, of the palace where he had spent so many happy years with his dead wife, Zenobia. She had been a slave in Nemedia, but he had made her sole queen over the green hills and golden fields of sunny Aquilonia. While she lived, he had—save for a few lapses while traveling afar—been faithful to her, no small feat for a rough, red-blooded warrior of Cimmerian lineage.

Since she had died in childbirth, he had resumed the habits of his days as a bachelor king, by keeping a harem of shapely concubines. The acquisition of these presented no difficulty. Conan's peculiar, highly individualistic sense of honor had kept him from ever in his life compelling a woman to submit to his embraces. On the other hand, there had always been plenty who were willing and eager to encounter this fate. But he had wedded no more wives; no woman had taken Zenobia's place.

Now that she was gone, he found himself often thinking of her, in moods of black depression that were unlike him. While she lived, he had taken her devotion as his due and thought little of it, as is the way of the barbarian. Now he regretted the words he had not said to her and the favors he had not done for her.

He found himself, too, thinking of old times and old friends. Faces out of the past thronged his mind: Bêlit, the pantherine, languorous pirate queen of the Black Coast, his first great love . . . Taurus of Nemedia, the fat old thief with whom he had sought to plunder the fabulous Tower of the Elephant . . . the enigmatic Stygian sorcerer, Thoth-Amon, whose trail had crossed his so often before that final, fatal confrontation . . . loyal, grinning Juba, the giant black from Kush with whom he had fought the men of the lost valley of Meru in the distant East . . . Count Trocero of Poitain, the shrewd banker Publius, the gallant soldiers Prospero and Pallantides—all friends who had come to his aid when the jealousy of King Numedides of Aquilonia had driven Conan into exile, and who had rallied to him when he led a revolt against the degenerate monarch . . .

Thus the faces of friends, lovers, comrades, and foes of his long past, which he would never look upon in this life, crowded upon him. The memories came back to him with increasingly poignant intensity, now that the bold, bright days of his reckless youth were long since over and gone and the Long Night was fast approaching. Well, he mused, age comes to every man if he lives long enough. And, by Crom, Conan would see one last sunset go down on a field of bloody corpses before the final hour of his life came upon him!

"Land ho!"

Sunk deep in melancholy, Conan had been leaning moodily against the rail of the poop deck, watching the morning sun climb out of the ocean through the eastern cloud banks. This cry brought him about, with the blood leaping in his veins.

"Whither away?" he thundered.

"Three points off the starboard bow, Captain!" replied the lookout from the foretop.

Conan clambered the shrouds to the maintop and searched the horizon ahead of the *Red Lion* with a fierce hawk's gaze. The West was still dark; but beneath the bands of cloud, to the right of the bow, a strip of more solid darkness lay along the horizon. Land. Pirates crowded the forecastle rail below, pointing and exclaiming as the shadowy bulk of hills loomed out of the morning mist. As Conan returned to the poop deck, Sigurd stamped up to join him.

"What is it, mate?" said the Vanr. "The Antilles at

last? By the sun disc of Shamash and the silver crescent of Demetria! Action at last! Gold and loot for all, and hot blood for sauce, by all the gods!"

Conan grinned. "Aye. Two moons aboard this craft, with naught but sea and sky around, seems like two centuries. But the voyage is over!"

Then came a wild cry from the lookout: "Dragon off the starboard bow! Coming toward us!"

Dragon? Conan felt a chill at the word. Then he froze, staring ahead to starboard.

Out of the unknown West it came, its spread wings and lofty curve of neck glittering with golden flame in the ruddy morning light, its mighty breast cleaving the smooth, oily swells. Eyes blazing with white fire and black smoke boiling from its flaring nostrils, it came across the waves at them out of the dim, foggy mass of the islands—a titanic winged serpent, mailed in gleaming scales, with eyes like globes of fire.

X. Dragon Fire

Submerged in red, tenebrous haze, where suns
  in sanguine splendor set,
Forgotten empires linger yet, like phantoms
  of forgotten days.
                    —*The Visions of Epemitreus*

"ALL HANDS ON DECK, with arms!" Conan's bellow, like the crack of doom, snapped his crew out of its wide-eyed trance, as the men watched the monster approach. "Archers to the forecastle! Yakov, signal when it's in range! Milo, man the catapult, with your squad! Aim it four points off the starboard bow. Steersmen, two points to port! Sigurd, shake out the mizzen; we may have to dance this ship around like a drunken Kothian peasant. Marco, fetch my helm and corselet to the poop!"

Then men scurried to obey with a clatter of weapons, sometimes punctuated by the clang of a dropped sword or pike. Up forward, the burly boatswain and his squad grunted and sweated as they levered the ponderous throwing engine into position, and others brought the tarry missiles up from the hold.

The *Red Lion* heeled and swung to port to bring the

monster in line with the catapult, since the engine was not pivoted and therefore had to be aimed by aiming the ship. The eyes of the monster, glaring like meteors, came closer and seemed to climb higher.

As soon as the thing came within bowshot, Yakov's squad sent a storm of arrows arching across the intervening water. Some stuck fast in the scaly hide; others glanced off the golden scales. But the monster seemed not to feel the hissing shafts. The clawed feet, on the ends of long, slender, birdlike forelegs, rising from the sides of its breast, did not twitch. The arched, swanlike neck did not writhe, nor did the snarling visage change expression. The golden mask came on, all glaring eyes and grimacing visage, filled with bristling tusks.

Then the sun, which had been hidden behind the eastern clouds, climbed out and shone upon the scene in its full glory. And Conan gave a shout: "That's not alive, men; 'tis a ship—a machine! Ready the catapult!"

For the sudden increase in illumination had shown Conan the truth. The "dragon" was a galley, like that which they had overcome in mid-ocean, but with its bow built up to resemble the front of a monster. The "wings" were two tall, narrow triangular sails, stiffened by bamboo battens like the sails of the ships of Khitai. These sails rose from a pair of masts in the waist, side by side instead of fore and aft as in most sailing vessels. Now the sails were trimmed to point straight aft, since the galley was rowing directly into the wind. Hence they contributed nothing to the ship's progress, albeit they did fortify the illusion of a winged sea monster.

A second volley of arrows rattled harmlessly against the bow of the dragon-ship. Conan saw that the "forelegs" were a pair of grappling devices, held up by cables over the water in front of the bow. When the vessel got close enough, these twin booms would be allowed to fall, and the "claws" would be driven into the woodwork of the *Red Lion* to hold her fast.

"Milo! Shoot one!" yelled Conan.

The boatswain signaled to the steersmen to bring the bow a little to starboard, so that his engine would bear. With a loud thump, the catapult released. The first of the balls of tar, trailing black smoke from its wick, arched across the water, glanced from the monster's neck, and fell into the sea.

Now the galley was a mere javelin-throw away. The curved breast of the dragon opened. A pair of doors swung wide, and a boarding plank extended itself out over the water. Inside the vessel, mustered at the base of the boarding plank, stood a fantastically garbed boarding party, bristling with weapons.

The ratchet of the catapult rattled as the crew desperately heaved on the windlass to recock the weapon. Then, *thump!* A second smoke-trailing ball flew over the water— right into the opening where the boarding party was mustered.

There was a burst of smoke, and a lurid light illumined the interior of the vessel. The boarding party milled in confusion; a couple of men fell or were pushed off into the sea, where the weight of their armor quickly dragged them under.

Smoke spurted from the hull of the dragon ship in a hundred places. The fire seemed to spread with preternatural speed. Faintly, Conan could hear the cries of trapped men. There was an impression of desperate efforts, half-seen through the breast-opening, to fight the fire. But soon flame spurted from the dragon's neck; then the wing-sails caught fire and blazed up . . .

"Amra!" screamed Sigurd. "Another one, to port!"

Conan whirled with a sulphurous oath. A second dragon-ship was bearing down upon them from the opposite side. Since this one was traveling with the wind on her beam, her wing-sails helped the oars so that she moved much faster than the first ship had done.

"Milo!" roared Conan. "Get that engine over to port!"

As the catapult crew struggled to lever their machine to the opposite side of the forecastle deck, the second dragon-ship quickly closed the distance. Conan swore at his own stupidity in letting the sight of the blazing first ship so rivet his attention that he had not been aware, until he heard Sigurd's bellow, of the approach of the second.

"Yakov!" he thundered. "Hold your shot until the doors open!"

This time, however, the dragon-ship did not open the doors to its boarding party so soon. Instead, it gave out a hiss as of a thousand kettles. From its open mouth, a tongue of liquid flame shot out. It formed a blazing arch across the narrowing gulf. It struck the side and deck of the *Red Lion*. In an instant, drops of the burning liquid were running hither and yon about the deck. In a panic, the pirates ran back from the rail, some of them beating at smoldering spots in their clothing. The liquid gave off a dense, black smoke with an oily smell. Conan guessed at once that this was a natural oil, like that which seeped out of the ground in the deserts of Iranistan and southern Turan.

But he had no time to explain this to his men. A second hiss, and another jet of liquid flame struck the foresail, which in an instant blazed up like a torch. The catapult crew and the archers scattered, screaming, as the sail flamed over their heads and showered the deck with bits of burning sailcloth.

"Hard to starboard!" yelled Conan. "Trim sail to run with the wind on the starboard beam!" For he saw that another flaming jet might destroy his mainsail and make the *Red Lion* a helpless hulk.

90

But it was too late. Again came the hiss and the jet, and the mainsail dissolved into a mass of leaping, thundering flame. The *Red Lion*, shorn of all motive power save the little triangular mizzen, slowed and wallowed. The grappling booms of the galley crashed down, driving their claws into the carack's deck. The doors opened, the plank extended, and the second boarding party rushed to the deck of the *Red Lion*.

These men had brown skins and slitted eyes, with knobby cheekbones and hawk noses. They wore bird-helms like those of the sorcerer on the green galley, and strange glassy armor over leathern jerkins. They carried curious weapons—swords with saw-toothed edges of crystal, hooked spears, and glassy globes held in slings. There were other weapons, which Conan could not, in the first moment, make out.

Yakov's archers should have met the boarding party with a deadly hail of arrows, but the archers had become as demoralized as the rest of the pirates. Conan roared and threatened from the poop, but still they milled and yammered witlessly in the waist. A few arrows whizzed into the boarders, but to little effect. The shafts splintered against and glanced off the fragile-looking armor of glass. A few of the crew mustered where the tongue of the boarding plank rested upon the *Red Lion*'s rail.

Conan leaped down the ladder from the poop deck, his great broadsword in hand, to add his weight to the defenders. The men of the boarding party, he now saw, bore curious equipment: tubes that ran from their nostrils, inside the glass helmets, to containers on their backs. It must, he surmised, be breathing equipment of some sort. But why?

The answer came just as he reached the main deck. The foremost of the attackers paused to whirl slings and shower his men with glass globes, each about the size of an apple. The globes burst with a musical tinkle and shattered into thousands of shining hards. Where each globe struck, a billowing cloud of pale vapor arose.

More and more of the globes smashed and tinkled; as fast as the wind blew away the vapor, more of the uncanny missiles renewed it. And Conan saw his men, milling about in the waist, sag and slump to the deck, unconscious. Down they went, man after man, until only a few still stood erect. The deck looked like a shambles, save that the fallen men lay peacefully and apparently unhurt, as if sleeping.

Then the boarding party swarmed down from the plank to the smoke-obscured deck, on which fragments of burning sail and rope still showered. With a challenging roar, Conan drove in amongst them, his broadsword weaving a shimmering web of steel around him. The crystalline armor splintered as the heavy blade struck it, shearing through glass, leather, flesh, and bone. Limbs were lopped off; howling cries of pain came muffled through the glassy helmets.

Conan hacked his way through the loose ranks of the first boarders, leaving three foes recumbent on the deck behind him. But others dropped down from the boarding plank to ring him round and return to the attack. He hacked his way through to the rail where, with his back protected, he won a moment's respite.

On the far side of the deck he saw Sigurd trading mighty blows with two assailants. Two more had already fallen at his feet. Then, although he did not seem to have been struck, the Northman dropped his scimitar and folded up on the deck, as had all the rest of the crew.

There was a sweetish smell in Conan's nostrils, and the world swam before his eyes. The attackers had given back before him, to form a semicircle hemming him against the rail. For three heartbeats, the Cimmerian faced his assailants, his gray-bearded lips bared in a silent snarl. Then, over the heads of the foremost attackers, several of the glass globes flew through the air, to smash on the deck at his feet.

Conan did not wait for the vapor to rise and drag him down. With a hoarse, gasping roar, he hurled himself against the semicircle. His broadsword, wielded in both rough, scarred hands, whirled about his head like the vane of a windmill. Crash! Crash! Two of the Antillians fell before his blade with heads or ribs crushed in. And then Conan was through the press and out in the open again.

He knew he could not fight the entire hostile crew single-handed. Though he might account for a few more, sooner or later they would surround him and cut him down. Already the fatigue of his years was weighting his limbs and slowing his movements. His breath came in gasps. The smoke and the whiff of the pallid vapor he had inhaled made him cough. Every one of his crew was now down—a few slain by the enemy's weird weapons, but the great majority felled by the vapor.

Another man might have been paralyzed by the problem of what to do next. The ship was plainly lost. Her deck swarmed with the boarders from the dragon ship. Her sails and rigging had vanished in flame and smoke; at that instant her fore yard, its sail consumed, crashed to the forecastle deck as the ropes upholding it burned through. A score of minor fires smouldered here and there about the deck, where pieces of burning sail, rope, or spar had ignited them. The first dragon-ship, which had been set ablaze, had vanished except for a floating patch of wreckage.

Conan saw that he could do his men no good by letting himself be slain or captured. If, on the other hand, he could escape, perhaps a chance would offer itself later . . .

The decisiveness of Conan's barbarian heritage decided his next actions without his consciously having to think about them or to weigh alternatives. With a final burst of strength, he bounded up the ladder to the poop deck. Of the two steersmen at the quarter rudders, one had disappeared; the other lay dead, while over the body stood one of the boarders with a bloody saw-edged blade in his hand. Conan rushed him and shattered the crystal blade with a single chop. A mighty thrust with both long arms sent the point of the broadsword crunching through the other's glass-plated mail shirt and through the man's body. Down went the man.

Then Conan dropped his bloody broadsword, doffed his horned helmet, and hurled it far out into the water. No use leaving any arms for the foe to salvage! He bent and tore from the head of the dead boarder the bird-shaped glass helmet and the breathing apparatus that went with it. As more Antillians stamped up the ladder to the poop deck, Conan settled the apparatus about his own head and shoulders.

The enemies rushed upon him with cries of rage. He caught up his sword just in time to parry the thrust of a wavy-headed spear, and a mighty slash smashed the helmet of the pikeman and the skull beneath it. Before any others could close with him, the Cimmerian sprang to the rail and dove into the heaving, blue waters. Carried down by the weight of his chain mail, he sank like a stone.

The morning sun, now high in the heavens, had burned off the last remains of the morning mist; the clouds dwindled and fled before its hot golden rays. Two by two, the boarders picked up the recumbent forms of the unconscious crewmen of the *Red Lion* and carried them over the boarding plank into the dragon-ship. Others busied themselves with putting out the many small fires, beating them with cloaks and dousing them with buckets of sea water drawn up by ropes.

At length, leaving a small prize crew aboard, the men of the dragon-ship returned to their own vessel. With a rat-

tle of gear, the boarding plank withdrew; the grappling
arms rose from the deck; the doors in the dragon's breast
closed. The dragon ship backed water with oars and sails
and maneuvered to bring her stern near the bow of the
Red Lion. Presently, with a creaking of ropes to trim her
sails to the following wind, the dragon ship forged ahead
in the direction whence she had come, towing the *Red
Lion* behind her.

XI. Terrors of the Sea

Bedight with tentacle and fang,
The monsters on the Lion sprang . . .
    —*The Voyage of Amra*

CONAN STRUCK the water with a mighty splash. Green waves closed over his head. Weighted by the chain mail that clothed his body to mid-thigh and by the massive broadsword in his fist, he sank like a stone.

The sea was cold; the morning sun had not been up long enough for its warmth to penetrate far below the surface. The bracing tang of cold salt water on Conan's limbs was not unwelcome. Salt stung his cuts and bruises, and the icy shock sent new vigor surging through his aching muscles.

He fell slowly through a world of pale jade green. As the hull of the *Red Lion* rose above him, he could discern the barnacles on her keel. Looking up, the old warrior saw two hulls above him—oval planets in a sky of shimmering, greenish silver. A weird sight . . .

His first impulse on hitting the water had been to strike out with his arms and swim. Then it came to him that the breathing apparatus in the crystal helm was designed, in some incomprehensible fashion, to enable him to breathe under water. Furthermore, he could see the sea bottom not far beneath his booted heels. At this point, close to the isles of Antillia, the ocean bottom sloped gently upward. Instead of falling into an ebony abyss of lightless gloom, he would descend only a few fathoms and then could walk to shore. So, controlling his instinct to swim, he permitted himself to sink to the bottom, treading water just enough to keep himself right side up.

Breathing was another matter. The helm came down to fit in saddle fashion over chest and back. Two glass tubes curved away over either shoulder to a tanklike affair on his back between his shoulders. The first tube entered the front of the helm on a level with his nostrils; the second, on a level with his mouth. A little experimenting showed that the wearer of the helmet was expected to wrap his lips around the lower tube, press his nostrils into the aperture of the upper, and then breathe in through the nostril tube and out through the other. When he exhaled, a column of silvery, shining bubbles rose from the apparatus with a gurgling sound. This unusual method of breathing took a little practice, but Conan got used to it by the time he landed softly, in a sprawling position, on the sea bottom.

The bottom was covered with fine, soft sand, which rose in little clouds as he scrambled into an upright position. Around him, the water was clouded with puffs and swirls of slowly settling particles.

Conan found that his vision through the crystal helm was good, except that beyond a few yards the water clouded and confused his gaze. Although there was enough light clearly to make out his nearby surroundings, the more distant hillocks of sand were drowned in a deep emerald gloom.

97

He oriented himself easily enough, since to follow the rising slope of the sea bottom he knew would lead him to shore. So he set off in that direction, laboriously plodding through the soft sand, lurching from side to side because his armor and the breathing apparatus made him top-heavy. Despite the weight of his mail, boots, and sword, his body felt peculiarly light. It was gripped with an even pressure, which exerted itself against his entire body surface. This made breathing a wearying effort. But, disregarding the difficulties of moving, he forged along with grotesquely slow strides, which lifted him clear of the ocean floor with every step.

Curious growths flourished on the sea bottom. He pushed through an enchanted forest of weird plants, whose long, silky fronds undulated like glistening, multicolored ribbons. Small, brightly colored fish darted about him like fantastic birds, flashing golden and purple and emerald and crimson and azure. Towers of pink and white coral rose about him, cloven and branching like petrified trees.

Passing through the coral growths, Conan emerged into an area of tumbled, upward-sloping rocks, which lay this way and that and leaned against one another like the ruins of some primeval city of giants. Clusters of sea creatures clung to them. Some were flower-like or star-shaped or covered with spines. Some had jointed legs and eyes on stalks; others thrust out branching, feathery appendages.

Pulling himself up from level to level among the tumbled boulders, Conan silently cursed as something sharp gashed one of his fingers. In time, he emerged on a level plateau and stood for a moment, resting.

The sun must be higher now, or else he had risen to a level quite near the surface, for the deep emerald of the depths had given way to a lucent chartreuse. By this clearer luminance he could make out another upward

98

slope, which must extend almost to the surface. In this slope gaped the dark mouth of a sea cave.

Eyeing the cave warily, Conan decided to give it a wide berth. His experience with caves on dry land had often proved them to be tenanted—and tenanted by creatures formidable to man. He was sure that things other than the bright, harmless little fishes dwelt in these liquid depths.

As he skirted the mouth of the cave, his eye caught a surge of motion in the darkness within. A spot of dim luminosity, as big as a serving platter, appeared, then another beside it. And something came sliding toward him across the sea bottom. It was like a ship's cable—or rather, like a tree trunk, covered with black, smooth, oily-looking bark, which had somehow been given flexibility and animation. The near end tapered to a slender whiplash, while toward the cave the tentacle thickened to the diameter of an old tree.

As the member writhed toward Conan, squirming and looping and rising from the sea bottom, he saw that its flat underside bore a double row of suckers, from little ones no bigger around than his thumb at the tapering end to others the size of horses's hooves further in. The thin end of the tentacle lifted from the sea bottom and tentatively touched Conan's boot, as if feeling this curious creature to see if it was edible.

"Crom!" gasped Conan, recognizing the tentacle as that of a creature of the kraken kind. He sprang backward, ripping his sword from the scabbard.

On dry land, such a leap would have taken him several feet back from where he stood, but things were different beneath the sea. Conan found himself floundering above the surface of the sand, turning end over end. Water leaked into his glassy helmet and gurgled in his ears as he revolved. With his free hand, he beat at the water to right himself.

The tentacle drew back. Then, like a striking serpent, it lunged up and out and coiled around his thigh.

Conan brought his sword down in a mighty slash. But the resistance of the water sent his stroke awry and robbed it of most of its force. The sword slightly gashed the rubbery tentacle and rebounded from it.

The grip on Conan's thigh tightened, until his leg began to go numb. His lungs labored against the pressure of the water. He struck again at the tentacle, only to have the water again weaken the blow.

The grip on his leg grew crushing; Conan became terribly aware of the giant strength in that coil. With desperate certainty he knew that unless he broke the hold of the sea monster, the tentacle would pull him down into the cave. There, in the center of the spreading circle of arms, a sharp, parrot-like beak and a rasping tongue awaited their feast.

The giant kraken was not yet fully aroused. It toyed lazily with its victim, sluggishly curious but perhaps not yet hungry enough. But now Conan saw another tentacle lifting into view, and yet another behind it.

He reversed his blade and thrust the point of the broadsword into the thick hide of the tentacle, just above the coil that was clamped about his leg. The point slowly sank into the rubbery flesh, until the blade transfixed the tentacle and came out on the other side. Thanks be to all the gods, he was armed with a straight, sharp-pointed blade, and not with a curved, blunt-ended scimitar or cutlass! Had the latter been the case, the epic of Conan of Cimmeria might have ended right there.

The sluggish kraken seemed hardly to feel the pain of its pierced limb. Conan sawed the blade slowly up and down. Suddenly he seemed to strike a nerve, for the tentacle whipped loose and lashed back and forth, hurling him head over heels through the water.

As he again settled to the sandy surface, another tentacle came snaking toward him, blindly questing like the weaving, bobbing head of some huge black snake. As it writhed past him, Conan brought the point of his blade down upon the limb, trying to pin it against the ocean floor. As the writhing arm rippled to one side, the point gashed it, sending it slithering back toward the cave, like a wounded serpent.

Now the water about Conan surged as the titanic octopus, fully aroused by the pain of its wounds, heaved its bulk out of the cave mouth. Conan gaped in awe at the size of the thing.

Counting its eight writhing arms, it was as big as a house. First came the tentacles, as long as the *Red Lion* and as thick at their bases as the trunks of century-old trees. They swept writhing out, seized boulders in their sucker grip, and drew the rest of the monster after them. The mouth with its beak was hidden from view beneath the circle of arms.

After the tentacles came the head with its two platter-sized eyes, mounted side by side above the bases of the forward tentacles. These eyes had slit pupils, like those of a cat, but the slits were horizontal instead of vertical. Their cold, lidless stare was one of the most unnerving that Conan had ever faced.

Behind the head came the bloated, baglike, limbless body, as big as one of the colossal wine vats in King Ariostro's cellars. Waves of changing color chased one another over the mottled mass: white, pink, russet, maroon, and black.

Conan stood motionless, debating what to do. He dared not flee down the broken incline at his back, because he would have to go slowly and would have his hands occupied and his back turned to the pursuing, angry monster. Conan guessed that it could not clearly discern him as long as he stood still. But if he moved, the motion would instantly draw the attention of the kraken.

On the other hand, he could not remain where he was, for the monster's present course would carry it close to him. As the octopus hunched and kedged its way forward, one or another of the lashing tentacles was soon bound to encounter Conan's body.

Choosing the simplest way of escape, Conan sprang upwards to get above the octopus. He hoped to circumvent it entirely and reach the upper slope beyond the cave before it sensed his location.

But Conan forgot that he was now clearly silhouetted as a black, moving object against the rippling, silvery plane of the sunlit surface above. Even as he swam above the brute, two questing tentacles reared up and closed crushingly about him—one about his waist and the other about his left foot. In that viselike grip he was helpless. In a few heartbeats, the tentacles would draw him down to the clashing beak . . .

Again Conan thrust the point of his blade against the thick, rubbery skin of a tentacle and pierced it. But the monster was not very sensitive to pain. Such was its vitality that he could have hacked through half its tentacles before seriously weakening it, and then it would have merely withdrawn to regrow its mutilated limbs. Conan felt the surge of titanic muscles in the crushing grip that held him helpless as, with inexorable force, the kraken drew him down toward its beaked mouth . . .

Then a bolt of black lightning struck and snapped through one of the tentacles holding him.

The dark shape had flashed out of dimness like a vast projectile. One snap of the triple rows of teeth had chopped a foot-long section out of one of the tentacles. The severed end uncoiled from Conan's midsection and drifted down to the ocean floor, flopping and writhing like a bisected worm.

The new arrival was a colossal shark, with a thick, tapering body over thirty feet in length. Dark slate-gray above, creamy white below, it banked and curved at the end of its lunge. For an instant it hung poised in the green waters. Then, with an arch of its supple spine, it curved about and came eeling back for another attack. Its small, yellow eyes, glassy with mindless hunger, glared into Conan's.

The Cimmerian was now held by a single tentacle, looped about his foot. Urgency lent extraordinary strength to his arms. Swung in both knobby hands, the broadsword sheared through the slender terminal portion of the tentacle, and Conan was free.

Not pausing to sheathe his blade, Conan swam furiously off at a tangent, striving to avoid the meteoric rush of the shark. The sword in his hand encumbered him and weighed him down on the right side, so that he slewed about in a wide half-circle. That was just enough to take him out of the path of the onrushing shark, whose triangular fins cut through the green-lit waters like plowshares.

It shot past him, its tooth-lined maw snapping shut on empty water. It missed him so narrowly that he could see the individual small, pebbly scales that crusted its rough, white underbelly as it raced by in front of his face. The displacement of the water tossed him about like a straw in the wind.

Then the shark turned and poised again at the end of its lunge. This time, Conan knew, he could not dodge. As the shark writhed toward him, three black tentacles flailed up past the Cimmerian and lashed about its bulky barrel, ensnaring the monster. The kraken's arms writhed like a nest of enraged serpents. The shark doubled, snapping furiously. Another tentacle was bitten in two, and the severed end sank writhing to the sand below.

But more tentacles whipped around the shark's body. Conan, holding his sword in his teeth to free both arms for swimming, saw what was happening as he stroked himself swiftly away from the combat. The octopus had thrown five of its eight arms—including even those that had had their tips severed—about the forward part of the shark's body and its head, covering its gills and its eyes. No matter how the shark blindly writhed and snapped, it could not bring its terrible jaws to bear upon its rubbery antagonist.

Meanwhile, the octopus had anchored itself to the rocks below by means of the suckers on its remaining three tentacles, to keep from being carried away bodily by the struggles of the shark. Sand, stirred up in clouds by the combat, obscured the spectacle. And then the water around the battle was plunged into darkness as a vast cloud of ink, ejected by the octopus, billowed up and out in all directions.

Conan was happy at this outcome. Engaged in fighting each other, neither the kraken nor the giant shark had time for him. He seized the opportunity to sheathe his sword and swim away from the scene of conflict. Before long, it vanished behind him in the dimness of the deeps, a cloud of deeper darkness against the gloom of the watery world. He never learned whether the octopus succeeded in smothering and destroying the shark, or whether the cloud of ink meant that the shark was winning and the octopus was seeking to cover its flight.

As he settled to the ocean floor a few hundred yards further to continue his progress on foot, Conan was just as glad not to know the outcome of the battle behind him. Ahead, up the slope, the bottom brightened as it rose to meet the surface of the Western Ocean. Conan plodded steadily forward, resolutely ignoring the pressure on his chest and the ache in his legs that came from the effort of dragging them forward against the resistance of the water. He still had a good part of a mile to go—perhaps even more—and he was eager to get out into clean, fresh air again.

He plodded slowly on through the dim waters, a weird, fantastical shape crowned with a glistening crystal helm, like some eerie god of the deeps.

XII. Lost City

Submerged in deep, red, mystic haze, where suns
   in sanguine splendor set,
Forgotten empires linger yet, like phantoms
   of primeval days.
   —*The Visions of Epemitreus*

CONAN HEAVED himself out of the waves and on to the lowest of the stone steps that led up to the sea gate, now closed for the night. From where he crouched, the setting sun had disappeared behind the crenelations of the towering sea wall.

Wearily, he pulled off the crystal helmet and its breathing tubes, whose supply of air was now exhausted, and laid the apparatus on the stone beside him. Then he tugged off his boots and poured the water out of them. For a while he sat hunched on the stone, glaring warily about him and breathing heavily. The task of hiking three miles over the bottom of the shallow, shark-infested sea, and then another mile along the shore to the city, had gravely sapped the old warrior's strength.

When he had reached the city in midafternoon, he had slipped back into the water. He waited, almost submerged, until all the small craft had tied up for the night, the sailrs had gone in through the gate, and the gate had closed, before daring to come closer.

Up and down the long, stone quays, which stretched north and south from the gate, several larger vessels were moored. Others rode at anchor in the harbor, but no life appeared on their decks. The crews either were below at their evening repast or had gone ashore. These Antillians, thought Conan, must either be careless or confident in their own strength, to post no watches on their walls and their ships at all times. Among the Antillian ships, the fire-blackened hull of the *Red Lion* lay half-submerged in shallow water.

Conan was not only tired after his day-long exertions but also ravenously hungry. As he sat under the darkening sky, he thought out his next step. Whatever it was, he had better be about it before some watchman stumbled across him.

His best chance, he thought, would be to get into the city. This would place him in a fearfully dangerous position. Not only would he be alone and friendless; but also he could not hope to pass unnoticed, because his height, color, and features distinguished him at the slightest glance from the small, brown Antillians.

Added to this was the problem of language. Back in his own world, he had a rough-and-ready command of a dozen tongues, albeit he had never lost the barbarous Cimmerian accent with which he spoke them. But the Antillians would use some speech of remotely Atlantean origin, long forgotten in Conan's world and changed in the course of eight thousand years out of all resemblance to any languages Conan knew.

Nonetheless, he could not lie here by the water's edge forever. Perhaps this evening hour, when the people were at their meals, would offer the best chance he could look for.

He rose and ran a hand along the stone of the forty-foot sea wall. The wall was made of huge, well-shaped blocks, worn by the salt spray of centuries. Between the blocks, the mortar had softened and crumbled out, leaving gaps into which fingers and toes could be thrust between the courses of stone.

As a youth, Conan would have faced the climb of such a wall without trepidation. Scaling sheer cliffs was a normal accomplishment of a Cimmerian clansman. But he had not had occasion to make such a climb in many years, and his grasp was not so strong, nor his movements so sure as formerly.

He pulled himself together, kicked the helmet and its breathing apparatus into the water, and tucked his boots through his belt. He was tempted to leave his mailshirt but decided to keep it after all. Doffing one's armor in the face of peril, merely to rid oneself of its irksome weight, was the act of a rash and foolish youth—not of crafty old Conan.

Then, digging fingers and toes into the cracks between the courses, he began to climb. Slowly, like some great tail-less lizard, he crept up the wall. More than once he felt a finger or a toe slip and almost resigned himself to a bone-breaking fall. But his grip held, and presently he squeezed through one of the embrasures of the battlement and dropped to the broad, level top of the wall.

On the other side of the wall, towards the city, a low parapet without crenelations ran along the edge. Crouching, Conan slunk across the wall to the inner side and peered over the parapet. The city lay spread out before him.

Near the wall, fishermen's hovels and sheds stood in the red glow of the sunset. Smoke from cookfires rose from the huts, and here and there fishermen were stretching out their nets to dry. Now and then a naked brown child ran on an evening errand. Beyond lay cobbled streets and a vista of stone houses, great and small.

The city was built on the sloping side of a hill. From where Conan crouched, he could see streets and squares, rising in tiers to the heights. The larger buildings were designed in a curious monolothic style, with thick, squat, tapering columns supporting heavy lintels and wedge-shaped corbelled arches. Walls of massive stone were dressed with stucco and plaster, either whitewashed or colored a violent crimson, a tawny cream, a bold canary, an emerald green, or a brilliant blue. The styling, although faintly reminiscent of nighted Khem or of the mysterious walled cities—some living, some ruined—that he had glimpsed years before in the deserts and jungles of the South, was strange to Conan's eye. It baffled him, as though built in accordance with an alien canon of aesthetics.

Higher on the slope rose stately edifices which were probably palaces, mansions, or temples. They had roofs of red tile or green copper and squat, five-sided towers with pyramidal tops. Conan saw imposing pylons, towering obelisks, and spacious gateways. Some avenues were lined with fantastic stone monsters.

Wall, cornice, doorway, architrave, and column capital were covered with leering, bug-eyed faces. Parrot-beaked, winged, or multilimbed beings of myth and legend sprawled in low, chiseled relief over gateways and walls. On some of the nearer walls, he could just make out rows of curious picture-writing. Composed of little squares containing weird faces and other elements, this form of writing was entirely new to him.

In the center of the city, amid a spacious square of level stone paving, rose a titanic pyramid with sloping sides, built of alternate blocks of block basalt and red sandstone. A lazy plume of smoke ascended from the topmost level, where Conan could faintly make out the outlines of a huge, flat altar. Flights of stone steps, guarded by stone monsters, rose up the side of the pyramid.

This structure exuded a sinister, disturbing aura of menace and terror, as if the mingled emotions of sacrificed thousands radiated from every stone. As he gazed at the accursed thing, Conan felt his skin roughen and suppressed a growl of hostility deep in his chest.

Few people moved in the darkening streets, increasingly drowned in purple night shadow. A few beggars slept in doorways. Here and there a yawning, sleepy-faced slave shuffled along on some errand for his master.

Conan waited until these few pedestrians were no longer to be seen. Then he took off his mail, made a bundle of it and his sword, and dropped the bundle to the ground below. The drop was considerably less than that on the seaward side of the wall. Then he swung himself over the parapet and began to descend, as he had ascended on the seaward side. Halfway down his grip slipped, and he kicked himself away from the wall as he fell, to land in a crouch on the turf fifteen feet below, jarred but unhurt.

A hasty glance revealed no sign that he had been seen, so he quickly donned boots, mail shirt, and sword. His only weapons were the broadsword and a broad-bladed dirk whose sheath was thrust through a slit in his girdle. These were not much with which to tackle a city full of implacable foes. But, with luck, daring, and the caution beaten into him by half a century of desperate adventures, he might have a fighting chance. And that was all he had ever asked of the gods.

Like a bronze shadow, he slipped between the hovels and across the first street into the shadows of an arcade. No eye marked his progress as he moved from column to gate, from doorway to pylon. In the daytime, the streets would be alive with a milling throng; now they were almost deserted.

In his shadowy progress through this silent city of gaudily-painted stucco over massive stone, Conan chose dark alleys and winding ways rather than the broad streets and wide ramps that climbed from level to level. He wondered where Sigurd and the pirates were—if they were still alive. Probably they would be immured near the Antillian equivalent of a slave market. In a strange city filled with enemies, where no man spoke a language he could understand, he had little chance of finding and freeing them; but he meant to try. Even in the lawless days of his early career, he had been noted for his fierce loyalty to his comrades.

Besides, if one man had no hope of prevailing against a city of twenty or thirty thousand, with sixty hardened fighters behind him the mathematics became a little better—not much, true, but sixty-odd men still have a better chance of winning out of a tight spot than one, even if that one be Conan the Cimmerian.

Conan's first problem, however, was to find a safe haven, a place of concealment. Where, in a city full of unintelligible foes, could he find an ally?

Then it would seem that he could count upon the favor of his barbaric gods, after all. He was slinking down a narrow street, lined with mean little one-room houses, when he heard a sharp hiss. As he looked around for the source, hand on hilt, the hiss was repeated from other directions. The faces of several women, dim in the dusk, had appeared in the doorways, and their hands beckoned to him.

In a flash, he realized that he had strayed into the Street of Harlots. He picked one door at random and strode to it. There was no time to examine the women closely in order to choose the most comely.

The harlot pulled Conan into her room. The cubicle was dimly lit by a bundle of rushes dipped in grease, set alight, and clamped in a wall bracket. She spoke to him in a stream of meaningless syllables, but the hand that she held out, palm up, was eloquent enough.

Conan pulled a small purse out of his girdle, took out a silver coin, and placed it on the outstretched palm. The woman held the coin to the rushlight, then squeaked with delight and threw herself upon Conan. She was plump, not unattractive, and clad in a simple cotton dress.

"Easy, lass!" he rumbled. "That coin should be worth several days' board, now shouldn't it?"

The woman fingered Conan's hair and beard and spoke again. This time her words bore a sound of disappointment. Conan guessed at her meaning.

"So you think I'm too old for such games, eh?" he said with a grin. "We'll see about that later. Meanwhile, by Crom, get me somewhat to eat, ere I starve!" By sign language he finally put his meaning across.

An hour later, he sat down to the meal that the woman, whose name was Catlaxoc, had prepared. She had gone out and returned with a basketload of provender, which she had cooked on her little hearth. She had not stinted on the supplies, and Conan dug hungrily into the large, strangely flavored roast fowl. The woman stood back, deferentially waiting for him to finish before eating herself.

"Now what," growled Conan, "is this thing?" He held up a cylindrical vegetable a foot long, on which grew rows of golden kernels. "And how in hell do you eat it?"

He finally made her understand that he wanted the name of the object. "*Mahiz*," she said.

"*Mahiz*, eh? Well now, show me how to eat it. Come on, sit down and eat, or I'll devour everything in sight and leave naught for you!"

At last he made his desires understood. Imitating the harlot, he gnawed the rows of kernels from the ear of maize, meanwhile asking for the names of the other edibles. By the end of the repast, he and Catlaxoc could exchange a few simple sentences.

Conan washed down the last of the meal with a flagon

112

of an unfamiliar fermented fruit juice. He belched and looked at Catlaxoc, who cast her eyes down demurely and smiled. Then she glanced significantly toward the alcove at the end of the room.

Conan grinned. "Well, 'tis true I am not so young as once I was, and I'm a little weary from a day of walking the ocean bottom and battling men, sharks, and krakens. But we shall see."

He rose, stretched, scooped Catlaxoc up in his arms, and bore her to the alcove.

It was several days later, in the evening, that Conan took leave of the harlot Catlaxoc. She clung to his arm, weeping, and he had to use gentle force to peel her off. He now wore the cotton cloak and kilt of a common Antillian. Catlaxoc had obtained this raiment for him and had also taught him the rudiments of the Antillian language. He knew that he was in Ptahuacan, the last surviving city of the Atlanteans on earth. His old garments and accouterments he had tied up in a bundle, which he carried by a sling over one shoulder.

He still dared not show himself abroad by day, since his size and his alien coloring and features would have made him a marked man in any but the dimmest light. But he now had a fair idea of the layout of the city and of the sort of disguise he would need to carry out his designs.

As the evening passed, Conan despaired of finding that which he sought. At last, as he stalked down a dark alley toward an open square, a huge figure, wrapped in a weird cloak of feathers, turned into the opposite end of the alley and came directly toward him.

Conan froze, then sprang upon the stranger like a striking lion. Before the man could utter a sound, Conan clubbed him into unconsciousness with a fist to the temple. He dragged the limp figure into a dark doorway, sweating a little at the nearness of the thing. One squawk from the robed giant, and Conan's enterprise might have ended right there.

He looked his victim over. Assuming the glass-mailed warriors on the dragon-ships to have been normal Antillians, this fellow was an unusually large one. Then Conan saw that the man wore built-up boots with seven-inch stilts for soles. To impress the gullible, perhaps? The fellow had the look of a priest or warlock about him: shaven pate, hands covered with talismanic rings, and chains of seals, amulets, and tiny idols strung about his scrawny throat.

Conan examined the man's hands. Aye, he must be a priest. No other occupation left one's hands so soft and uncallused.

The man was curiously clad. Beneath the feather robe, his lean, brown body was nearly naked, save for a tight skirt of pleated cotton. Thick bracelets of gold, worked with complex cryptic glyphs, encircled his wrists, arms, and ankles. The feather robe, the like of which Conan had never seen before, included a plumed cowl. The robe was of coarsely-woven wool, covered with feathers whose bright hues could be discerned even in this faint light. The quills of the feathers were drawn through the coarse weave of the wool and fixed in place with small, individual knots. A lining of a thin, finely woven crimson stuff resembling silk kept this rough, prickly surface from scratching the wearer's body.

It struck Conan that if he donned the robe without the built-up boots, he would be only a little taller than the priest-magician. In fact, with his arms hidden and the cowl pulled up around his face, he might be able to walk abroad without attracting attention. But even the cowl would not be enough to hide his unclipped gray mane and beard, which contrasted with the smooth face and shaven pate of the priest.

Conan solved this problem by tearing off a length of the

114

silky red material and winding it about his hair and the lower part of his face, concealing all but his eyes. Then he struggled into his boots and mail shirt and hung his sword at his side. He donned the heavy, hot, prickly feather robe and pulled the cowl close about his face.

He had no way of judging the effect, but it seemed likely that that he could pass casual scrutiny. His blue eyes and the red scarf about his chin might still attract attention, but he shrugged off this possibility. In his experience of city life, a priest or a magician was unlikely to be meddled with by common folk, who were usually only too glad to avoid men of these classes.

Gathering his courage, Conan strode boldly forth into a square lit by the moon and by torches set in brackets on the walls of the surrounding buildings. Almost at once, his disguise was put to the test. A potbellied shopkeeper, who was just putting away his display of goods for the night, confronted him first. The little brown man was placing his stock of ornaments of copper, jade, silver, and gold and his collection of feathered headdresses in a set of wooden caskets. As Conan strode into view, the feathered robe swirling about his booted ankles, the shopkeeper glanced sideways with black, frightened eyes at the towering, faceless figure. Then he bowed and, snatching up an amulet of jade that dangled against his breast, kissed it obsequiously and remained in this servile position until Conan had passed.

So Conan had survived his first test! Obviously, the little folk of Antillia went in great fear and awe of their priest-wizards. With reasonable care and luck, he stood in little danger of challenge.

For hours, Conan explored the broad ways and winding alleys of Ptahuacan without arousing any special interest. Priests in such feathered robes were evidently a common sight along the high-walled, cobblestoned streets of the lost Atlantean city. Later, when the streets became wholly deserted, he found an empty, tumbledown hut and slept until dawn. Then he set forth on his explorations again.

In the morning's light, Conan saw dozens of other tall, feather-robed figures stalking about on stilt-soled shoes. They strode grandly through the crowds, never deigning to reply to the humble greetings of those they passed. It would seem that the priest-wizards of old Atlantis were the rulers of this city, also.

It would also seem that the populace was entirely subordinated to them. To Conan the people seemed a listless, downtrodden lot, with glazed, indifferent eyes and frightened faces. With apprehension in their dark eyes, they scurried out of the path of the tall, feather-robed priests, whose arrogant authority Conan strove to imitate.

Ptahuacan, Conan found, was built on ascending levels, and the parallel streets that ran along these levels were connected by sloping ramps and stairways. The city was a remarkable technical achievement, denoting a sophisticated culture with ancient traditions and well-developed artistic canons. The stonework was equal to anything Conan had seen in his own world; even the modern cities of his realm could not match the massive proportions of the mighty temples or the meticulous precision of their masonry. The fantastic, temple-crowned ziggurat in the central square, as large as any of the pyramids of Stygia and reminiscent in its style of the fanes of some of the sinister cults of Shem, must have taken centuries of labor by thousands of workers to erect. Around the margins of the square ran a set of stone benches, rising tier upon tier until they could have held thousands of spectators facing the pyramid.

Conan stayed out of the square of the pyramid, for it seemed to be a holy place. He might well encounter many priests garbed like himself, who would not be timid about accosting him. So far, he had been able to dodge the feather-robed ones he saw in the streets. They did not seem a very companionable caste anyway. Aloof, unapproachable, and busy on their own unguessable errands, they rarely stopped to speak even with one another.

Conan spent much time in loitering near groups in order to hear something of the language. It was guttural and sibilant, given to long word-units. He could now understand many isolated words and a few phrases, but a long sentence spoken rapidly baffled him. Although its grammar seemed utterly different from that of any of the languages he knew, a few of the words he had learned from Catlaxoc did bear a faint resemblance to the corresponding words in his native Cimmerian.

It occurred to the old Cimmerian that the Atlanteans—who rose to civilization after the fall of Valusia, much of whose culture they adopted—were in part the ancestors of his own people. In the little-known era before the Cataclysm, the tribes and clans of an elder Cimmeria had warred and intermarried with the Atlantean colonists on the Thurian coasts. Many Cimmerian tribes, half-civilized through long contact with Atlantean colonists, had served Atlantis as mercenaries in the final centuries before the island continent sank beneath the sea. As the Cimmerian barbarians acquired the rudiments of civilization, they borrowed words to express more complex concepts from their ancient enemies. Hence, some faint resemblances lingered between a few words of similar meaning on both sides of the vast Western Ocean. Such resemblances, however, were not enough to give a stranger from across the sea a command of Antillian speech without much arduous practice.

From the occasional overheard word or phrase that he could understand, Conan grasped that the main topics of gossip in Ptahuacan that morning were two. One was the combat between the dragon-ships of the Sea Guard and

117

the alien vessel from parts unknown. The other was the blasphemous assault upon one of the holy priests, who had been incredibly robbed of his sacred feather robe. Conan listened eagerly for news of the whereabouts and fortunes of his crew; but, if any speaker knew the answer to that question, he did not say.

While Conan was loitering near crowded market stalls in one of the larger bazaars, the chance that he had awaited presented itself. A sly-eyed little man in a tattered kilt lingered with elaborate casualness near the copper-bound box where a fat merchant kept his trade metal: slugs of lead, rings of copper and silver, and quills of gold dust. Even as Conan glanced, he saw the little man dip one bare, scrawny arm into the box with the deft speed of a striking serpent. In the blink of an eye, the man had removed two quills of gold dust.

The merchant, engaged in a voluble exchange with an aristocratic customer, who leaned from a slave-borne palanquin to haggle over a fine pelt from some large, catlike beast, saw nothing. A grin of joy wrinkled Conan's hidden features as he watched the thief glide away, the precious quills vanishing into his kilt.

As the thief slunk from the bazaar, Conan quietly followed him into an empty alley. Then in one lithe bound he was upon the little Antillian, who squeaked like a frightened mouse when Conan's massive hand clamped on his bony shoulder. Conan fended off the stroke of the needle-like little obsidian dagger that had appeared from thin air. He seized and squeezed the man's hand, and the glass-bladed knife tinkled to the slimed cobbles.

As the little thief raised fearful, curious eyes to the giant in the feathered cowl, Conan growled in broken Antillian: "Take me to king of thieves, or I break your arm!"

At last the dice were rolling in his favor. Like all cities, great Ptahuacan must have a criminal underworld. And, if one is in trouble with the ruling class, one can always find a welcome amongst the worldwide guild of thieves!

XIII. Thieves of Ptahuacan

Black evils essence hither comes from some
   unknown dimension far,
And those who leave earth's gate ajar shall die
   as earthly life succumbs.
                    —*The Visions of Epemitreus*

CONAN'S CAPTIVE led him by winding ways into the more
sordid sections of the ancient city. Here, homeless dere-
licts and filthy beggars lounged in crumbling doorways.
Raddled whores leaned from windows to compete for the
trade of an occasional passerby.

As he penetrated the slum area, Conan began to realize
the unthinkable age of the city. Here the stone steps and
ramps were worn into sloping saddles by the tread of
countless generations. The very stone of the walls was
worn slick by the brushing of millions of shoulders. Ages
of wind and rain had eroded much of the stone into po-
rous, crumbling ruin. Long abandoned and tenanted only
by vermin, many structures had collapsed. Whole blocks
of houses lay in mouldering ruins in this, the most ancient
sector of the city. Grass grew between tilted paving stones,
while weedy trees sprouted amidst the tangles of long-

overgrown gardens and courtyards. If the sight of a feather-robed priest-wizard in these shabby streets was unusual, none of the inhabitants gave evidence of this fact. For, as Conan passed with the weasel-faced little thief in tow, hardly one raised curious eyes. It seemed to be the custom in these parts of Ptahuacan ostentatiously to ignore the doings of others, probably as a means of self-preservation. Doubtless this was the thieves' quarter, where lawlessness flourished.

Only when they neared the headquarters of the thieves did Conan realize that his progress had been under sur-veillance all the time. As they passed down a crooked alley between walls that leaned awry, two burly figures, armed with cudgels, appeared in front of them, while another pair closed in from behind. They were all big and stout for Antillians and naked except for soiled, apronlike garments of patched leather. Fixing Conan with cold, somber black eyes, they advanced from either end of the alley toward the place where he stood with his captive.

Conan let go the thief in order to put a hand on the sword hilt under his robe. The little thief moved away a pace, then turned to spew a volley of abuse, too fast for Conan to follow.

"He grabbed me after I lifted some gold dust from Hatupep's stall," cried the thief. "I know not what in Hell's name he wants, but—"

"Ease off, Itzra," growled one of the bullies. "We'll find out what he wants." Advancing on swift feet, he lifted his copper-bound cudgel.

Conan laughed and threw back his feathered robe and cowl. His broadsword hissed from its scabbard. The bul-lies stopped as if they had run into an invisible wall—but not, it seemed, from simple fear.

"Lords of Hell—iron, or I'm a blind man!" gasped one of them.

Another muttered an expletive and peered more closely

120

at Conan, observing with wonder his height, his unshorn mane and beard, and his smouldering blue eyes.

"Gods of death, what *is* he?" the fellow swore. "No such man has ever been seen in all Antillia!"

With his back against the wall, Conan barked a laugh, swinging his blade from side to side to menace all five hoodlums.

"One who stole this robe from its owner, friend, and no spy for your rulers, if that is what you think!" he rumbled. "Moreover, one who would see your chief on business, to profit of both. And I *will* see him, whether you like or not!"

He held his sword level so that the daylight flashed from its blade. The four guards and the cutpurse gave back, eyeing him with growing alarm. Strangely, his sword seemed to arouse more interest than he himself did. Conan guessed that for some reason—perhaps lack of ores in this island chain—ferrous metals were virtually unknown here, although legendary tales of the iron and steel of ancient Atlantis had been handed down through the generations.

"Now," he grunted, "will you take me to your leader, or would you rather fight?"

They were happy to oblige.

The local underworld lordling was an enormously fat man named Metemphoc. His face was a bulging mass of lardlike flesh in which a pair of cold black eyes glittered like fragments of polished obsidian. His mouth was a thin-lipped gash across his round, brown face; his nose, a mere blob between his swollen cheeks.

His headquarters was a series of abandoned cellars beneath the ruined houses at the end of a filthy alley. The walls of stained, crumbling plaster were hung with gorgeous tapestries of strange design, and on the cement floors were scattered elaborately woven mats and the tanned skins of beasts of many kinds. Silver thuribles filled the air with rich incense. The quiet luxury and gilded splendor of Metemphoc's apartment contrasted vividly with the squalor of the exterior.

Like a fat toad, Metemphoc lay wrapped in gorgeous brocade amidst a nest of cushions as he listened to Conan's tale. His face impassive and his black eyes coldly glittering, he uttered no word until Conan had finished his account. Then a long, suspenseful moment stretched on while Metemphoc examined Conan from head to foot, paying almost as much heed to the sword that lay across the Cimmerian's knees as to the man who held it.

With a sigh, Metemphoc rubbed fat jowls with pudgy fingers, whereon sparkled a king's ransom in gem-studded rings. He laughed throatily and called for wine and meat. The suspense broke.

"By the gods of stealth, big man!" he chuckled, "old Metemphoc has never heard such a tale in all his poor, sick days; therefore it must be true! Aye, with that barbarous mane and uncouth face fur, and those uncanny sky-colored eyes—and, ahem, an accent such as these tired old ears can barely understand—this fat old man has no choice but to believe that you do, forsooth, hail from an unknown land to the east. Notwithstanding that our beloved masters, the holy priesthood—ha!—inform us that naught lies thither but a wild waste of waters, with never a speck of land."

They amicably toasted each other. Conan gulped thirstily at a sweet, pungent wine such as he had never tasted. Doubtless, he thought, this drink was fermented, not from grapes, but from some unfamiliar local fruit.

He felt quite at home. By pure instinct, he and the toadlike master thief understood each other. Although born thousands of leagues apart and of alien cultures, they spoke the same lawless language in their hearts.

While they drank, food was brought and set out on the low table between them. Conan dug hungrily into the reast. Besides the Antillian foods with which he had already become familiar, there were nuts and berries of a dozen kinds. The repast ended with a curious, large, prickly fruit with a spray of sword-shaped leaves growing from its top. Metemphoc cut it into ring-shaped, yellow-green slices. Conan found the taste startling at first but not bad after a few bites.

Meanwhile they carried on a desultory conversation between mouthfuls. Metemphoc said: "Aye, I know of that strange ship, full of barbarous foreigners, which our Sea Guard captured a few days past. That is one reason I was willing to believe your tale."

"Are my men still alive, and if so where?" grunted Conan.

"They live, or did last night. They are in a dungeon below the Anteroom of the Gods—that gray citadel that stands on the edge of the Square of the Great Pyramid."

Conan reflected that the wily underworld princeling seemed willing to give him the information he sought, frankly enough; but almost visibly his cold, clever mind was searching for a mode to make a profit from the stranger. He did not trouble to conceal this from Conan, who fully grasped the thoughts that raced behind the impassive façade of the man's fat face.

"What will be their fate?"

"They are held for sacrifice, in the temple atop the Great Pyramid."

"Eh?" Conan made a sudden movement, spilling some of his wine.

"Why, yes. They will be given to the demon-god Xotli, in accordance with the rituals that have come down from ancient Atlantis . . ."

Conan's nape hairs bristled as Metemphoc explained, with unruffled aplomb, the customs of the local priesthood. Before the fall of Atlantis, the priests of Xotli had been a powerful faction, who worshiped their demon-god with awful rites of blood and terror. When the High Gods had destroyed Atlantis for its sins, the priests of Xotli and their slaves had fled from the sinking land in a mighty fleet of flying ships powered by the mysterious force called *vril*.

Conan had heard vague rumors of these Atlantean sky ships. He understood that, with the passage of centuries, the ships had worn out, or their supply of power had failed; and the secret of their manufacture had been lost in the ages of barbarism and bloodshed that followed the Cataclysm. Therefore no such ships existed in Hyborian times.

The priests of Xotli, continued Metemphoc, had ventured southwest from the doomed continent. They made a landfall in the little-known island chain they called Antillia. This consisted of seven large islands in the Western Ocean between Atlantis and a much larger continent, sometimes called Mayapan, still farther west. When the Atlanteans landed, they found the islands in the possession of a race of small, brown, slant-eyed savages, similar to the people of Mayapan. They easily conquered these natives and reduced them to the same slavery as the servants they had brought with them. In the millennia since the Cataclysm, the blood of the Atlanteans and of the aboriginal Antillians had mingled, until today the islands were inhabited by a single, mixed race.

Since the original conquest of Antillia and the construction of great Ptahuacan, the Xotlian priesthood, under the hereditary Hierarch of the Sacred Mysteries of Xotli, had ruled with an iron hand, despite occasional outbursts of rebellion on the part of their subjects. The hierarchs had kept the masses under control by telling the people that all lands—even Mayapan—had sunk with Atlantis, and the world was naught but a waste of wind-tossed waters. stretching from Antillia in all directions to the rim of the world, where sea met sky and the stars rose out of the foam of the endless seas.

"Do you believe this?" said Conan.

Metemphoc chuckled. "If a priest asked me, I should say yes. Most of the people believe, or at least lack the guts to question the teachings of their masters. But, between you and me, some of us know that Mayapan still stands; and now your coming has shown that land still exists on the other side of the waters, also."

"Why do the priests proclaim this lie, when they know better?"

"It helps to keep their subjects under control. If they believe there is no other land they could flee to, they will despair of escaping from the iron rule of the priests of Xotli."

"Tell me of this demon-god and his rites."

Metemphoc explained that Xotli, Lord of Terror, was a demon-god of the Elder Night. He appeared unto his worshipers as a roiling cloud of ebony darkness, a vortex of ultimate, boreal cold like that of the winds that blow between the stars. He drank the living souls of those slain upon his towering, pyramidal altars. To sustain the linkages between the Hierarch of the Mysteries in this world and the Demon of Darkness in the nighted depths of its unknown dimensions beyond the universe, the raw life-force of the victims was projected into the other worldly abyss.

Calmly, the fat master thief told how naked captives by the thousands were immolated atop the sky-reaching black-and-crimson zikkurat that Conan had glimpsed amidst the upper tiers of the ancient city. There, on the altars of Ultimate Night, the priest-wizards tore open the breasts of the living victims, ripped out their hearts with knives of volcanic glass, and offered up the life-force thereof to the whirling cloud of vampyric darkness that

125

formed above the pyramid and hung there for hours, feeding on the living force of human souls. The corpses they dropped down a shaft into some unknown pit or cavern.

Conan growled, and his eyes flashed dangerous fires as he listened. The mere idea of human sacrifice did not especially shock him. He had seen too much bloodshed in the course of his long life, and such practices were not unknown among the nations of Conan's own world in the Hyborian Age. But that his own friends and followers should be offered up in such barbarous rites—that was something else!

He sloshed down a mouthful of the pungent wine. "What then of the Red Shadows?"

Then Conan learned that the population of Antillia had become so depleted by the constant sacrifices that the wizard-priests had been forced to travel far afield to secure an adequate supply of captives to slake the dark thirsts of Xotli. First they raided the shores of Mayapan; then, when the coastal natives of that barbarous, sparsely peopled land scattered into their impenetrable forests, the priests had begun to reach out in other directions.

"The Red Shadows, as you call them," said Metemphoc, "are the spirit-servants of the Dark One. I had not known until now that the Hierarch (may his spirit be reborn in a tapeworm!) had been raiding the unknown lands to the east. Black Xotli must be hungry indeed! Our own sacrifices have grown so numerous of late that the city is half empty, as you have seen. Whole squares and streets are depleted of people. Thousands have fled to the hills or to the adjoining isles; but the rule of the priests extends thither, too, and they hunt them down. That is the reason for the Sea Guard, which seized your own vessel. It watches the harbors to intercept any who, doubting the word of the priests, essay to flee to some hoped-for land beyond the seas."

Conan's gaunt, scarred hands opened and closed on

emptiness, as if they clenched a human throat between them. "Now I understand the Red Shadows," he growled. "From what I have seen of sorcery in my own world, I know that once a dark force from beyond has obtained a foothold in the world of men, it needs ever-growing numbers of sacrifices to sustain it. The demons of the Elder Dark are—I know not how to put it in your tongue—they are negative; not nothing, but *less* than nothing. Life-force streams in to fill the void of their false existence. But their vacuum can never be filled and needs ever more and more life-force to sustain their illusion of life. Do you understand me?"

"I do," said Metemphoc. "Go on."

"Why, man, do you know that, unchecked, the servants of Black Xotli would ravage all the lands of this world until the very planet is empty of man? Nay more, they would then seize upon all higher forms of animal life, to leave the world to the fishes and the worms. It was this whereof the shade of Epemitreus sought to warn me—this perverted form of worship that should have sunk with Atlantis, eight thousand years ago."

"From what the ghost of your wise man said," replied Metemphoc, "it would seem that the gods have chosen you to stand between the world of living men and the Shadow of Evil. Only you can tip the balance between life for the world and death."

"Aye," muttered Conan. "But *how*?"

XIV. The Black Labyrinth

Red eyes flamed as the blood-mad horde
From the ebon mouth of the tunnel poured.
White fangs gleamed in the cavern black,
As after him swarmed the chittering pack.
                              —*The Voyage of Amra*

Down the dark tunnel went Conan. Stalactites hung
down like stone drapery from the arched ceiling far above;
an occasional drop of limewater fell from their tapering
ends. The cavern floor was scummed with mud and be-
slimed with the calcareous drippings of the mineral
growths above. Here and there, the growth rose from the
floor in glassy humps and soaring pillars, where stalagmites
had formed.

The cold, moist air reeked with strange, repellent odors.
A faint, sour breeze blew in Conan's face. Guided by it,
the old Cimmerian paced through the black labyrinth,
which stretched for miles beneath the age-old city of Ptahuacan.

Old Metemphoc, the master thief of Ptahuacan, had
flatly told Conan that by no conceivable route could a single armed man gain entry into the triple-guarded citadel

where Conan's Barachans lay immured, awaiting the Day of Sacrifice two days thence. Countless guards, gates and doors, locks and bars lay between the open streets and the secret heart of the priestly fortress.

Conan's agile mind, however, was not so easily lulled into abandonment of his design. In response to his endless queries, the Lord of Thieves bethought him of the ancient labyrinth of caverns and tunnels beneath the city. Whence they had come, no man could say. But the city was built upon a massive outcropping of limestone, and perhaps ages of erosion by underground streams had hollowed them out.

The thieves well knew the tunnels of the highest level and used them often. But the deeper tunnels were shunned even by them; for doubtful, hair-raising rumors circulated of strange cries from these noisome depths, of shambling forms half-glimpsed, and of men who, having dared the deep tunnels, cried out and then vanished forever.

Under Conan's implacable questioning, Metemphoc had reluctantly owned that the deep tunnels might well connect with the dungeons of the Vestibule of the Gods. Still, he had urged Conan to find some more wholesome way into the forbidden citadel. But Conan had proved obdurate to all his well-meant urgings.

At length, Metemphoc had seen that Conan was adamant in his determination to try to rescue his comrades by means of the deep tunnels. With a heartfelt sigh, the fat master thief then called his henchmen into conference. They began to riffle through the archives of the thieves' guild. Ancient maps of the labyrinth of tunnels were unearthed. Conan pored over these, memorizing the twists and turns of the caverns and the landmarks by which he could find his way.

So here was Conan, stalking through the darkness of the deep tunnels, scrambling and leaping over irregularities in

129

the floor of the cavern. In one hand he bore a lantern furnished him by the master thief. This device—a fine example of Antillian technical skill—was a little bronze lamp with a cylindrical reservoir for oil, a spout from which projected a sputtering wick, a disk-shaped reflector of silvered bronze behind the flame, and a handle in back. From long polishing, some of the silver had been worn away from the face of the reflector, revealing the bronze beneath. But the little lamp was still useful for Conan's purposes. It would, Metemphoc had said, burn for several hours before its fuel was exhausted.

Here and there among the branching mouths of the tunnels, a white mark was blazoned against the wet stone. These were the thieves' blazes. Where none was visible, certain odd configurations of stone had been described to him as landmarks—for instance, a humped shape of limestone that looked like a gigantic spider.

Conan moved steadily ahead, though he little liked the cold, damp breeze that wafted upon him from the unseen depths. As he moved, his mind could not help conjuring up strange pictures from the odd sounds that wailed and echoed and whispered about him in the darkness. Now and then he heard a weird, sobbing cry, which rose to a piercing shriek of inhuman agony and died away again to a faint moan, like the wind through distant pines.

At other times, he thought he sensed the stealthy tread of unseen feet about him, in the unlighted mouths of side passages and in the main tunnel behind him. Sometimes whispered words or cold, mocking laughter roused atavistic fears of the supernatural in his barbaric soul—fears which he crushed with iron self-control.

Then, too, there came to his keyed-up senses a soft, slithering sound, as if some titanic worm or slug were crawling over the rough stone floor. Even so seasoned an old warrior as Conan could not help a shiver of revulsion as he thought of what creatures might dwell in these sun-less depths, far beneath this forgotten city of Time's Dawn.

The moans and wails, he sternly told himself, were simply the sounds of wind blowing through the mock-forests of limestone formations. The laugh was the gurgle of underground waters, distorted by the conformation of the tunnels. The crawling sound might have been the slow, creaking subsidence of the very earth itself. But still the superstitious fears arose in his mind to plague him.

The skin of Conan's nape prickled. From somewhere, he was conscious of the gaze of unseen eyes. He had been winding his way through the subterranean caverns for—he thought—well over two hours. He had slipped and staggered on wet stones, stumbled over irregularities, leaped ditches and chasms athwart his path, bumped his head on low ceilings, squeezed through narrow places, and scrambled up and down steep slopes. He had disturbed colonies of bats, hanging upside down in clusters from the overhead. They squeaked angrily at him and whirred away into the darkness.

He wondered how much longer his lamp would continue to give light. It seemed to him that already its flame had weakened; it sputtered and wavered, as though its supply of oil were coming irregularly.

And now the barbarian's keen senses, but little blunted and dulled by years of urban life, told him that he was under the surveillance of hidden eyes.

He slowed his pace and went forward cautiously and silently. His keen eyes searched the dark mouths of the caverns about him for hidden agents of the Antillian priesthood, but he saw no sign of men. Nevertheless, his wilderness-trained senses told him that the pressure of an unseen gaze rested upon him. He wondered if the Antillian priesthood possessed crystal globes of magical powers, which they had inherited from their Atlantean forebears and the like of which he had seen in the Hyborian lands, whereby an initiate magician could observe events taking place afar. Were the cold eyes of an Antillian watching his every move, right now?

He froze and held his breath, listening. Far behind him sounded a metallic clang, as of a gate opening. Had he imagined it?

Now sounds grew behind him. Sweat started from his skin, for the sound was a muffled squeaking, pattering, and rustling. It was as if the unseen watcher had loosed behind him a horde of small but formidable animals, to hunt him through the cavern world and pull him down with thousands of claws and teeth.

Now the sounds grew louder and clearer. Conan muttered the name of Crom, half a curse and half a prayer. Now he believed that, in truth, those tunnels had been barred by unseen grills, and that some watchful guard had perceived his stealthy approach and loosed the slithering horde to overwhelm him.

Conan swung his lantern to illumine the main tunnel behind him. The light was reflected redly from hundreds of pairs of small eyes close to the ground. As the living flood of pursuers came into the stronger light, Conan almost dropped his lantern in astonishment. The pursuers were rats—but what rats!

Conan had become familiar over the years with the little gray rat of the Hyborian lands, and the agile black rat of Vendhya, and the burly brown rat of Hyrkania. But these animals overtopped the rats of his world as normal rats overtopped mice. They were as big as large cats or small dogs, weighing several pounds apiece. They were not only huge, but gaunt as if half starved. Their white chisel-teeth snapped on empty air, hungry for his blood and flesh.

Conan whirled and ran, his thudding boots keeping time with his laboring pulse. Against such a bloodthirsty horde, his sword could do little; the greatest fighting man of his age would have gone down in seconds under the tide-of squealing, snapping rodents.

So Conan ran as he had never run in all his life—even on that unforgotten day and night nearly fifty years before, when he had escaped from the Hyperborean slave pen, after battling his way to freedom with a length of broken chain, and had fled through rain and snow with a pack of famished wolves at his heels.

Now the breath seared his lungs with every gulp of air, as if he inhaled the breath of a furnace. His heart pounded against his ribs. His laboring legs seemed weighted with lead; his muscles ached as if devils were piercing them with fiery needles. But still he reeled and staggered on. The wind of his motion bent back the little flame of the lamp until it was in danger of being blown out altogether.

Behind him, the rats scuttled and bounded and galloped, keeping pace with him. From time to time one of the foremost would jostle or tread upon another, and there would be a brief exchange of squeals and bites. But the rest of the horde flowed on, little delayed by these brief eddies in its course.

Then Conan's eyes caught a faint glimmer ahead, and the murmur of running water told him that he neared a river. As he approached, he saw that it was a rushing torrent of black water. For an instant he hoped that it would prove narrow enough to leap and thus form a barrier between himself and the pursuing horde. But then he saw that, at least right here, it was over twenty feet wide—too great a distance for him to leap. Long ago in his lusty youth, if not exhausted by running and not burdened by weapons and armor, he could easily have made such a jump. But now . . .

With widespread legs, Conan faced the furry onslaught. His chest heaved and his panting lungs drew in the cold, dank air, now fetid with the stench of the horde of rats. The headlong race through the black caverns had set his heart to pounding furiously and the blood to coursing madly through his veins. While the blood still roared in his ears, he drew his broadsword for one last, great fight.

For nothing that lived could survive close combat with this horde of blood-mad, rustling rodents. All his life, Conan had only asked for a fighting chance, and now he did not have even that. But, if he had only moments left to life, he would live those moments to the full and go down fighting. For all his years, he was still in splendid condition and could have broken the backs of men half his age. And if no mortal eye should witness the last stand of Conan the Cimmerian, at least the gods would relish the spectacle—if indeed the gods looked down upon men and watched over them, as those lying priests maintained.

Conan stood on a roughly triangular ledge of rock that jutted out into the underground river, like a miniature cape or peninsula. Hence the rats could not come at him from the sides or rear, although they could still attack him on a broad front.

The giant rats poured out of the mouth of the tunnel like a river of black-and-gray fur, their eyes twinkling redly in the lamplight like the stars of some infernal dimension. Their squeaking chatter rose above the murmur of the river, and the rasp of their claws on the stone was like the hiss of dry, dead leaves whirled by an autumn gale.

Conan stooped to set down the little lantern behind his feet and gripped his sword in both hands. He raised his voice in a booming battle song of his barbarous people, and then the rats were upon him.

As the first one came within reach, a slash sent it flying in two halves over the heads of its comrades. Then, for long minutes, the heavy broadsword whirled like the vanes of a windmill as Conan struck right and left in a deadly figure-eight pattern, his point just clearing the ground with each stroke. And with each stroke, one or more rats went flying—sometimes whole, sometimes as separated heads, bodies, limbs, and entrails. Blood splashed Conan's arms and legs. Now and then he miscalculated so that his point touched the stone in its sweep, striking sparks.

But on pressed the horde, as those behind pushed those before them into the whirling blade. Now the press loosened somewhat, for some of the rats turned from the attack to feast upon the mutilated remains of their dead brethren. And still Conan swung and sent rat corpses flying by the score. His blade was now red halfway to the hilt, and the stone underfoot became sticky and slippery with blood. With each stroke, his sword threw off a spray of red droplets.

Now they pressed upon him again, and for all the slaughter he wrought upon them he could not hold them back. Some dug their chisel-teeth into the tough leather of his boots. Furiously, Conan kicked and stamped, crunching the life out of those that swarmed around his feet; but others quickly took their place.

A rat scrambled up to the top of Conan's boot and bit through the cloth of his breeches at the knee, inflicting a flesh wound. A quick slash sent the rat spinning away in two halves. Others gained his waist and breast, but their attempts to bite were foiled by the mail shirt. One made a great leap from the ground, landing on Conan's chest, and scrambled on up towards his throat. Conan snatched it away just as its whiskered muzzle touched his flesh. He grabbed at those swarming up his body, hurling them against the tunnel walls or into the river behind him.

But they were gaining upon him. Rat corpses lay in heaps about him, and he stood on an uncertain footing of mangled, furry bodies, split entrails, and rodent gore. Although his boots and mail had so far protected him from all but a few minor bites, both knees bled from nips, and the left hand with which he seized rats that climbed his body streamed blood from several gashes.

Then the rats gave back for an instant. Panting, Conan glared around. In his desperation, he saw something that he would have noted sooner, had he not been so closely pressed. A bowshot downstream from where he stood, a natural bridge of stone spanned the rushing black water. Instantly he realized that, if he could gain this arch, the rats could come at him only two or three at a time. On such a narrow way, he could hold out against the horde indefinitely.

To think was to act. With a surge of power, he rushed towards the bridge, wading through swirling masses of rats and crushing the life from one with every bound. Others leaped upon him to scramble and bite, until his knees streamed blood and his breeches hung about them in tatters. But such was his impetus that he reached the bridge before the rats could pull him down.

Gasping for breath, he staggered out upon the arch of stone and took his stand in the middle, where the footway narrowed. He regretted that in his haste he had not taken time to fetch the little lantern with him; but its fuel must be nearly exhausted anyway. From a distance it still shed a faint, pulsating light upon the scene.

It took the rats only a few heartbeats to perceive him, but the pause enabled him to catch his breath and clear his head. He felt his age in laboring lungs, aching thews, and pounding heart.

Now they came on again. As they flowed up the slope of the arch, Conan confronted them, crouching with his sword in both hands. As they came nearer, he began methodically slashing, right-left-right-left, each blow hurling rats off the narrow way. They died by scores and hundreds. Those that were merely knocked off fell splashing into the stream below, which swiftly bore them away into the darkness. Small, furry heads bobbed in the flood, circling to get their bearings and then striking out for the nearest shore until the darkness swallowed them up.

Never in all his years of war and slaughter had his sword taken so many lives. If the rats had been men, Conan's stand upon the underground river would have depopulated a whole nation. Like a tireless machine, he fought on . . .

The end came quickly. A huge black rat with bristling whiskers—a grandfather of all rats, weighing over ten pounds—came bounding from the squealing pack to leap at Conan's gasping throat. Conan was long past feeling. His arms were numb and as heavy as lead, and the pillars of his spread legs seemed like cold columns of iron. With his left hand he snatched at the furry body as the rat dug its sharp claws into the links of his mail and lunged for his jugular vein. But strength was draining from Conan's limbs; he seemed unable to tear the creature loose, even when its sharp chisel-teeth gashed the skin beneath his beard.

As another rat attacked his boot, he kicked out at it, missed, and staggered back, followed by a worrying mass of rodents. As he brought his heels down heavily to keep from falling off the arch, the natural bridge broke beneath the weight and the pounding. With a loud crack, the whole center section on which Conan stood fell straight down into the flood with a tremendous splash.

Conan found himself under water, carried down by the weight of his mail. The gigantic rat that had been worrying his throat was gone, but Conan now faced the prospect of ending his land stand by drowning.

With a thrust of his legs against the bottom, he fought his way up to the surface and gasped a lungful of air before the weight dragged him down again. The swift current bumped and banged him against the irregularities of the bottom, rolling him over and over. Once more he fought his way to the surface. He had always been a splendid swimmer; but now the mailshirt, which he had retained through such peril and which had protected his torso from scores of bites, was dragging him down to his doom.

Once more he fought up to the surface. Once more he took in a straining lungful of air. And once more the weight drew him inexorably under. His consciousness was slipping away, as though he were falling into a deep, dreamless slumber.

XV. Dungeon of Despair

In vain the Lion fought and fell—
His crew already gazed on Hell . . .
—*The Voyage of Amra*

SIGURD OF VANAHEIM was disgusted. When the stout old
Vanr, like the rest of the *Red Lion's* crew, had succumbed
to the narcotic vapor released by the men of the Antillian
dragon-ship, he hardly expected ever to see daylight again.
But Death had withdrawn its black claws from the fallen
warrior. Not this time had Sigure met his bane.

Instead, dazed and confused, the old pirate had awak-
ened with sharp, aromatic fumes in his nostrils. He found
himself in the capacious hold of the Antillian vessel, amid
his Barachan shipmates, who were also returning to consciousness. They were surrounded by small, brown, grinning warriors in weird glass armor.

As Sigurd slowly recovered his wits, he saw that the
dragon-ship was not really built from gold or some other
yellow metal, but was just thinly plated with it. The
planking under his feet was of good, solid wood, seemingly as hard as oak and of a darker color. Wooden bulk-
heads and hull planking surrounded him. To his ears came

the muffled thunder of waves breaking against the curved hull, and Sigurd knew what must have happened.

His eyes searched the faces of his crew. They were battered and bloody, and a couple bore bad wounds. But nearly all of them seemed to be present and alive, even if prisoners in the hands of the Antillians.

A pang went through the old freebooter's heart. Anxiously he searched the faces of his men again—but where was Conan? The familiar scarred, frowning face under the iron-gray mane was not to be seen.

Sigurd's heart sank as a doleful expression clouded his ruddy features. He well knew the iron courage of the old Cimmerian; few men, during Conan's long life, could boast of having taken him alive. Fiercely attached to his freedom, the old gray wolf might well have preferred to go down fighting rather than to be taken prisoner by these doll-like little brown men. And, if Conan were indeed among the slain, then upon Sigurd's bowed head devolved the awesome responsibility of command.

"Courage, my hearties!" he rumbled. "Belike we be free men no more, but we still live. And whilst we draw breath, sink me for a lubber, but there's always a chance of fighting our way to freedom!"

Goram Singh probed him with large, somber black eyes. "Where is the lord Amra, O Sigurd? Why is he not amongst us?" the Vendhyan demanded.

Sigurd slowly wagged his graying red beard. "By Shaitan's tail and the star of Ningal, comrade, I know not. Mayhap he is in another part of this cursed galley . . ."

The Vendhyan silently nodded, but he bowed his turbaned head and avoided Sigurd's eye. He knew as well as the Vanr that Conan would probably not have been chained apart from the rest. More likely, the mighty Cimmerian had gone down to the cold halls of the restless dead with an Antillian glass sword in his vitals.

The voyage to the harbor of Ptahuacan took them nearly an hour, what with the extra weight of half a hundred burly pirates in the hold. Sigurd blinked in the sunlight as they were led out of the gold-sheathed dragonship in heavy glass chains. Curiously, he peered at the vista of the ancient city of weathered stone and gaudily painted stucco, rising tier upon tier up the slope of the mountain.

Never in all his days had Sigurd of Vanaheim seen so strange a metropolis, whose every building was covered with sculptured friezes of monster-headed gods and animal-headed men, with monolithic gateways of solid stone and strange rylons climbing into the bright morning sky. Over all, the cryptic and ominous shadow of the vast, black-and-crimson pyramid shed a pall of gloom. Rising from the temple on its top, a perpetual plume of smoke streamed from the structure as from a man-made volcano.

The pirates, however, caught only a brief glimpse of the ancient Atlantean city. Their guards led them briskly through the city streets, up the stupendous ramps from tier to tier, and through the bronze gates of the gray citadel adjoining the square of the great pyramid. When those mighty gates clanged to behind their backs, the pirates saw their last of open air and blue skies for many a long day.

Guards herded them down endless stone stairs, which coiled deeply into the bowels of the mountain on whose side Ptahuacan was built. When their knees, aching from the interminable descent, seemed ready to collapse under them, they came at length into a tremendous chamber cut from the solid stone. Here their shackles were unlocked while they stood, guarded by alert wardens with leveled, glass-headed pikes.

Next, their ankles were secured to a long chain of glass, which ran through looped rings set into the stone wall. Although they had a little slack—enough to move about and lie down—for practical purposes they were confined to an area extending a few feet from the wall.

Then the guards filed out, and the captives were left in solitude.

In this huge room, vast stone columns, like the trunks of gigantic trees, rose to support the roof. They seemed to be part of the natural rock and to have been left standing when the rest of the chamber was excavated, to provide support for the roof.

Far above their heads, plates of shiny metal were set in the ceiling. By some forgotten Atlantean science or wizardry, these plates glowed with a soft, ruddy light, shedding a wan illumination upon the chamber beneath. Sigurd wondered for an instant whether these plates were made of the rumored Atlantean metal, orichalcum, but he had too many other things of more urgency to spend much time with this surmise.

Once a day the captives were fed. Buckets of a greasy, tepid stew were dumped into a long, foul, stone trough than ran along the wall behind them. The stuff was lumpy with cold grease and stretched out with some unpalatable meal. But hunger soon overcomes squeamishness, and Conan's crew came eagerly to await the feeding hour. It took all of Sigurd's authority to keep them from fighting over this unappetizing swill.

Immured in this dank place, far from a sight of the heavenly bodies, the pirates lost all sense of time. Had they been here hours or days? They argued endlessly among themselves over this question, until Sigurd roared: "Shut up, all of you! Ye'll drive me mad with your clack. We can be pretty sure they feed us at the same time every day, so each feeding marks one day. Yasunga, ye shall be our timekeeper. Find a place on the wall and make a scratch there for each serving of this slop."

142

"But Sigurd," complained a small Ophirean, "we know not how many days have passed up to now. Some say four, some five, some six or seven. How shall we know—"

He broke off as the Vanr, shaking huge fists in his face until his chains rattled, roared: "Shut up, Ahriman blast you, or I'll wind a chain around your scrawny neck and tighten it until your lousy little head comes off! Every man can add his own guess to the number of days shown on Yasunga's tally, and it matters not a damn anyway! And the next man who raises this question, I'll smash his skull like an egg!"

"Ah, eggs!" said Artanes the Zamorian, a stout-bellied bull of a man renowned among the pirates for his appetite. "What I could do with a couple of dozen fresh fowl's eggs . . ."

They grew matted with filth. Their untended wounds either festered or scabbed and began to heal. Two died: a burly Shemite, who had taken a cracked skull in the battle, died screaming and fighting invisible foes. The other was a stolid black from the steaming jungles of southern Kush, whose tongue had been cut out by Stygian slavers before he had escaped to the Baracha Isles, and who perished from a fever. Both bodies were taken away by glass-mailed Antillian guards for some unknown disposal.

With the help of Yasunga the navigator, Milo the boatswain, and Yakov the bowmaster, Sigurd did his best to keep his men in order and their spirits up. This was not easy, for they were a motley lot, given to irrational grudges and hatreds, outbursts of violent passion, superstitious fears and crotchets, and sudden fits of gloom, despair, or quarrelsomeness. And Sigurd, while a mighty man whose name commanded respect among the Red Brotherhood, lacked the aura of invincible luck and supernatural power that accompanied Amra the Lion.

The best way to keep them interested and out of mischief, the Northman found, was to encourage them to talk about their exploits of the past. So they reminisced for hours, arguing point by point through battles, sieges, and forays in which they had taken part.

Again and again they recalled the deeds of Conan—or Amra the Lion, as most of them knew him. They told and retold how, at the sleek side of Bêlit, his first great love, he had plundered the Black Coast and ventured deeply into the unknown jungle rivers of the South, where the she-pirate had come to a grisly doom in a ruined city of stone. They told how, a decade later, he had reappeared out of nowhere to sail with the Barachan pirates, and how still later he had cut a swath as captain of a ship of Zingaran buccaneers. Again and again they recalled the fantastic career of their chief, the hero of a thousand perils and the victor of a thousand fights, from single duels to earthshaking battles.

At length, even Sigurd's spirit began to fail. The dark, dank dungeon with its silent stone walls, the pall of gloom that weighed down their spirits, and the threat of an unknown doom all spread a mood of sullen, hopeless depression heavy enough to bow down the brightest spirits.

Several times Sigurd, with the help of the strongest men in the company, tried to break the chains that bound them. The links were fashioned of what looked like fragile glass—but no glass he had ever seen was as tough as this transparent material. It was as strong and unyielding as bronze. No amount of pulling, pounding, stamping, twisting, or jerking did more than slightly mar its slick, iridescent surface.

No, escape appeared to be beyond their powers. They could only wait for doom to strike in its own good time. And, at last, strike it did.

The metallic clash of spears on shields aroused Sigurd from uneasy slumbers. He started up from the straw to see the room filled with small, flat-faced soldiers and to see his comrades being prodded into wakefulness and their hands being bound behind them.

"What is it, Captain?" muttered Goram Singh.

Sigurd shook his head, so that the unkempt, graying red beard wagged. "Crom and Mitra know, shipmate!" he growled. Then he raised his voice: "Look alive, lads! Straighten up and show these brown dogs we be men, even though kenneled here in our own filth like beasts. If it be the executioner's block, then by the green beard of Lir and the red heart of Nergal, we'll show these stinking pigs how men can die, eh lads? Be ye with old Sigurd to the last?"

His exhortations raised a ragged cheer from the pirates, who croaked: "Ay, Redbeard!"

"Good lads, all! And mayhap 'twill be only the slave-dealer's mart, eh? With the luck of the Brotherhood, I think such lusty lads as we will be purchased by high-born ladies, for special service in their boudoirs!" He gave an exaggerated wink.

The men responded with a chorus of catcalls and obscene jests. Sigurd grinned and chuckled, but it was all pretense. For he thought he could guess the terrible end that awaited them, here among the black-hearted heathen of these cursed islands at the edge of the world.

Sigurd was right. Blinking blearily in the unaccustomed sunlight, the pirates gazed around them, awestruck at the spectacle. Above soared the blue vault of heaven, like a sapphire dome in some palace of the gods. The sun stood almost overhead, blazing down upon them with a furnace-like heat that was welcome after the cool darkness of the stinking dungeon. They drank in the fresh sea breeze from the harbor, knowing that it might be their last chance in this world to draw a lungful of salt air.

They had issued from the portals of the grim, gray citadel called the Vestibule of the Gods into the square of the great red-and-black pyramid. The pyramid towered up in front of them, over the heads of the thousands of Antillians who thronged the square.

At the head of the line, Sigurd looked back upon his comrades. They were a sorry-looking lot, ragged and filthy, with long hair and matted beards. Ribs showed through the holes in their tattered shirts from the meager, unwholesome diet.

Ranks of soldiers kept a lane open through the throng from the Vestibule to the base of the pyramid, and along this lane the pirates' guards prodded their captives until they came to the tail of a line of naked Antillians.

Priests in feathered robes and stilted shoes, towering over the throng, bustled officiously about, while others stood in ranks at the base of the pyramid, holding up curious standards and banners.

The pyramid loomed above them now. Whips sang and cracked over the bedraggled pirates' shoulders as the soldiers herded them into place at the end of the file of naked Antillians. The latter toiled slowly, silently, and unresistingly up the steep stone stair that climbed the near face of the zikkurat.

Sigurd tipped back his head, gazing through slitted, watering eyes at the top of the pyramid and trying to see what was happening there against the glare of the noonday subtropical sky. He made out a great black stone altar and, next to it, a tall throne on which sat a feather-robed figure.

One by one, the silent Antillians were led with bowed heads to the temple at the top. Sigurd could see beast-masked, feather-robed priests seizing them by the arms, cutting their bonds, and stretching them on their backs on the stone. Then another figure stepped forward in an even more fantastic costume of plumes and jewels, although it was too far to make these out clearly. He ex-

146

tended a gaunt, brown arm to trace some cryptic symbol on the naked chest of the supine Antillian. Then . . .

Sigurd's eyes suddenly watered, and he lowered his head to wipe them. When he could look up again, it was to see the arm of the high priest raised with something in its fist —a knife that glittered like glass. The knife descended in a sharp arc. The figure on the stone gave a convulsive jerk. For an instant the hierarch bent over his victim, sawing with his knife and groping with his free hand.

Then the lean, crimsoned brown arms rose again, lifting against the bright sky a dripping, crimson mass—the heart of the victim, cut from his body while he was still alive.

The assembled thousands gasped. The priests set up a low-pitched chant, swaying in time to their slow, hypnotic song, which reminded Sigurd of the rhythmic murmur of the sea. The sacrificial fire next to the altar gushed dark smoke as the heart of the sacrifice was added to the many already heaped upon the glowing coals. The corpse was dragged away beyond Sigurd's vision by the crimson-splashed attendants, and the next silent victim was led forward. Numbly, Sigurd wondered how long this grisly rite had already been going on.

The guards urged the line forward another step. The pirates behind Sigurd were as silent as he, struck dumb by the terror that lurked above them on the pyramid. The old freebooter felt nothing but a cold emptiness, as if time had stopped and the universe had shrunk to the dimensions of his own body. A few moments more and all would be over, the long voyage ended, the tale told. And what did it all matter? Was every human life as meaningless as his had proved to be? And yet . . .

Within his bristling chest, Sigurd's stout old heart surged with abhorrence. His manhood revolted at this spineless submission to fate. Was he no better than these dwarfish islanders? By Thor's hammer, no! Death he did not fear. He and it were old shipmates. What, then, was the gust of revulsion that rose within him? Pride! Aye, by Badb and Morrigan, that was it; sheer pride!

Sigurd gave a bark of laughter that brought looks of wonder and surprise to the faces of the pirates nearest to him in the slow-moving line. Aye, this was a *Hell* of a way for an old Vanr to die!

XVI. In the Dragon's Lair

> He hears the scrape of scales on stone,
> And Amra learns he is not alone . . .
> —*The Voyage of Amra*

AT FIRST he thought he was dead—that the sea of life had washed his waterlogged corpse up on the lightless shores of the afterworld. For a time he lay still, only blinking his eyes to clear them of the water that blurred his vision. Then, little by little, his senses awoke, and Conan knew he had somehow survived.

Incredibly, he still lived. By all odds he should be a corpse, drowned by the weight of its mail shirt, rolling and bumping along the bottom of the swift stream.

He levered himself up on one elbow and stared around him. He lay in another vast cavern; and, curiously enough, it was not altogether dark. As his vision cleared, he made out thousands of little points of glowing green light on the distant walls and ceiling of the cave. For a fleeting instant he thought he was lying out of doors, and that the green glows were stars; but then he realized that no stars would be all of the same brightness or so uniformly distributed.

He lay in wet, gritty sand on the shore of the subterranean river into which he had fallen. The river entered this cavern from a low, arched entrance, which he could dimly discern across the rushing water. The channel made a sharp bend, angling off to the left to vanish through yet another dark portal. The abrupt change of direction must have thrown his nearly lifeless body against the slope on the outer side of the curve, and some lingering spark of animation within him had forced him to haul himself the few feet further up the slope necessary to drag him out of reach of the torrent. Then he had collapsed into complete unconsciousness.

He heaved himself into a sitting position and examined himself as well as he could in the faint, green glow of the cavern walls. No bones seemed to be broken, but he was covered with minor cuts and bruises, where the teeth of the giant rats or the stones of the river bottom had marked him. His breeches were in shreds, and his boots had been slashed and gouged by the rodents' teeth until his gnarled toes and ankles showed through the rents. Luckily, the cold water of the underground river had washed his wounds clean.

A fine film of rust had already formed on the links of his mail shirt, so that the garment emitted a faint squeal as he moved. He still had his dirk, but his sword he had lost when he fell into the flood.

He tottered to his feet, staggered, and recovered. Every muscle in his mighty body ached. His battle with the rats had strained even his iron stamina almost beyond the limits of endurance. He had almost gone into a trancelike, berserker state of insensibility. Then, while he was still exhausted, he had come within a hairsbreadth of drowning. No doubt he had slept a whole day and a night, and perhaps longer.

As he gingerly flexed his stiff muscles, he became aware of the prickly pains of returning circulation. At the same time, renewed vigor surged back into his battered hulk. As he stalked back and forth on the crescent-shaped beach, his limbs limbered up. He cast off the empty scabbard of his broadsword; too light to make an effective weapon, it would only encumber him.

He was, he realized, hungry and thirsty. The thirst he quenched at the marge of the stream, but there was no way to satisfy his ravenous hunger. If only he had carried one of the giant rats down with him to devour . . .

A pale blur of motion beneath the surface of the stream caught his attention. Then he saw another and perceived that there were fish in the river. He found an outcrop of rock that would serve as a convenient platform and settled himself upon it, watching the water with the patience of an old hunter.

Time passed. Then a sudden lunge of Conan's long arms, and his hands came out of the black water clutching a wriggling fish by the gills. He brained the fish against the rock, scraped off the scales with his dirk, and ate the firm, white flesh raw. When he had finished, he washed the blood and scales from his face and hands in the stream and set about exploring.

First he headed for the nearest wall of the cavern, moving cautiously and peering ahead of him warily, lest he step into some trench or pit, or fall down a shaft leading to a lower level of caves. Although the light was dim, many hours in darkness had made Conan's eyes sensitive to the faintest illumination.

Arriving at the place where the cavern floor curved up to join the wall, he looked at the nearest of the green glows that spangled the cavern walls. It seemed to come from some luminous object about the size and shape of a child's finger. Too cautious to touch unknown objects with his bare flesh, Conan drew his dirk and prodded the glow with the point. The green thing squirmed and fell from the wall, rolled past his feet, and set off at a brisk crawl across the floor of the cavern. A closer look showed Conan that the source of the light was a luminous grub or caterpillar of some sort. Hundreds of thousands of the creatures clung to walls and ceiling.

Conan gave a grunt of satisfaction. Instantly, hundreds of the glowworms nearest to him on the cavern wall went out, leaving a large patch of blackness. Conan remained quiet, staring, and presently the hundreds of little green glows returned, faintly at first and then brightening to their normal luminosity. Sudden sounds evidently frightened the worms into turning off their lamps.

The light was convenient, but Conan realized that by now he must be far off the track he had originally set himself. While fleeing from the rats, he had taken whatever path seemed to offer the fewest obstacles, heedless of the route he had so carefully memorized with the help of Metemphoc the master thief. There seemed to be no hope of retracing his steps and again picking up the thread of his original route. Even if he could somehow get back up the underground river, he might find the horde of giant rats still lingering where he had left them. And now he did not even have a sword to fight them off with.

He explored the vast cavern further. Titanic stalagmites rose here and there from the rocky floor to approach and sometimes to join with stalactites descending from above. These natural pillars reminded Conan of the columns of primitive temples to the gods of the underworld. Their immensity dwarfed even his giant form.

Now that his hunger was somewhat appeased, he gave thought to procuring a more effective weapon than the dirk. Although this was a stout and formidable dagger, he felt he needed something with more reach, for there was no telling what other nameless denizens of the underworld he might meet in his subterranean wanderings.

Stalagmites, he observed, were all rounded and blunt at the upper end. Wanting something he could use as a spear, he chose a slender stalactite instead. He picked up a loose lump of limestone, weighing perhaps twenty pounds, and swung it against the tapering shaft. The stalactite broke off; Conan dropped the piece of limestone and caught the falling stalactite. At the boom of the falling lump, half the glowworms went out and then slowly returned to their normal brightness.

He hefted his new weapon. It was a four-foot shaft of stone, as thick as his wrist at one end and tapering to a point at the other. While the point was not so sharp as that of a real spear, it would still pierce the body of a foe when backed by Conan's still-powerful muscles. It could also be grasped by the small end and swung as a club, although Conan entertained doubts of the strength of the material. It could even be thrown as a javelin for a short distance.

Thus armed, Conan felt fit to challenge even the nameless terrors of this dark realm. Cautiously, he began exploring again, in the direction in which the cave seemed to extend the farthest.

As he walked, the cavern narrowed and the ceiling became lower. The glowworms became fewer, so that in the increasing gloom Conan was forced to move warily, probing ahead of him with the stalactite lest he fall into some hole. His position was hazardous enough as it was, without the additional discomfiture of suddenly finding himself plunging down some well or shaft hundreds of feet deep.

As it was, he stumbled over an irregularity in the cavern floor and bumped into a stalagmite about his own height. The slender stone column broke off and toppled over with a loud boom, which reverberated in the confined space. Instantly every nearby glowworm winked out, leaving Conan in virtually complete darkness.

"Ahriman eat these accursed caves!" he growled. He continued in the direction in which he had been headed, feeling ahead with his feet and with the point of the stalactite.

Then his outstretched club touched something that moved. Conan froze motionless, straining his eyes and ears for some clue to the nature of the invisible being in his path.

A loud hiss came from the darkness before him, like the hiss of a serpent but magnified many times over. A rank, reptilian odor filled his nostrils. He would have noticed it sooner but for the faint breeze that blew against his back and hence wafted the stench away from him until he was almost upon its source.

Sweat started on Conan's brow. Had he stumbled into a nest of snakes? Like most northern barbarians, he detested the snakes that swarmed the jungles of hot southern lands. Several times in his career he had experienced close calls with serpents far larger than any of the common species—monsters over fifty feet long, with heads as big as those of horses.

Thinking silently to withdraw, he took a step backwards. Then came a scraping sound, as if some heavy weight were being dragged across the stone before him. Conan halted and held his breath lest the slightest sound betray his presence.

Then the glowworms began to light up again. As their faint, greenish radiance suffused the tunnel, a well of cold, green light appeared in front of Conan, on a level with his own eyes. It was a huge eye. Then it swung to one side, and Conan saw that it was one of a pair.

As the glowworms again reached their normal level of illumination, Conan saw that he had encountered a dragon—a reptile similar in general outlines to one of the large, edible lizards he had seen on display in the butcher shops of Ptahuacan. But this was a fifty-footer. Its jaws opened slightly, revealing the gleaming sabers of its curved white fangs. From the tip of the tapering head, a forked, snakelike tongue flicked out, wavered in the air, and was withdrawn, testing for the scent of the being who had aroused it.

Conan whirled and ran headlong through the gloom, seeking a way around the giant reptile. The dragon raised its scaly body off the rock where it had been resting and started after Conan, its bowed legs swiveling outward in an awkward, mechanical-looking gait that nevertheless covered the ground with ominous speed.

In trying to circle around the dragon, Conan found himself headed down a side passage. The glowworms were fewer here, forcing the Cimmerian to proceed cautiously; but far ahead appeared a stronger light. Moreover, its color was not the emerald green of the glowworms but the neutral shades of ordinary daylight.

Behind him, the dragon's claws scraped loudly on the stone with each stride, while the scales on the lower side of its tail hissed as the member was dragged along over the rough stone floor. In the open, Conan thought he could outrun one of these reptiles; but here he had to watch his every step lest he take a tumble and be snapped up by his pursuer before he could rise again.

The tunnel he was traversing widened into another chamber, and the light from up ahead waxed a little stronger. It was strong enough for him to see, in plain sight, two more dragons, one on either side. One was asleep, while the other was finishing a meal. A quick glance showed Conan the nature of the meal: a pair of human legs dangled from the creature's jaws.

As Conan dashed between the two monsters, the sleeping one opened its eyes. The other made a gulping motion, whereupon the human legs slid a little further into its jaws and out of sight. Had both reptiles been alert and unencumbered, they could easily have caught the Cimmerian by a quick sideways lunge of their huge, scaly heads as he passed.

As it was, the pursuing dragon, uttering a deep, sonorous grunt or bellow, clattered into the cavern between the two others. Soon all three were in pursuit of Conan. The one with the man in its jaws gulped frantically to down its morsel so as to have its gullet free for another one.

This cavern was a kind of anteroom to a still larger chamber, illuminated by a narrow shaft of daylight that came down from a hole in the ceiling. The chamber, which had apparently been enlarged by the hand of man, was roughly square. At one side rose a pair of huge bronze doors, like those which Conan had seen on the front of the great stepped pyramid in the main square.

On the other side, a set of spikes had been driven into the stone wall, forming a kind of ladder that extended up from the floor to a height of thirty feet. Here was a small platform, which opened into a tunnel. Conan had a fleeting impression of an armed Antillian lounging on the platform, but he had no time to observe the man more closely now.

His main attention was on the six slate-gray dragons, ranging from a mere pup ten feet long to a hoary old sixty-footer, in the middle of the cavern floor. They squatted in a circle, with their heads inward and directly under the shaft overhead. Their heads were raised, each scaly muzzle pointing upward toward the opening through which the daylight filtered, as if engaged in some mysterious reptilian worship of the ancestor of all dragons. Jagged crests of keeled scales ran down their backs from behind their heads to the ends of their scaly tails.

Now Conan's lungs were filled with the stifling musty reek of the reptiles' bodies. Amid the filth that covered the floor of the chamber, Conan glimpsed the leathery surfaces of half-buried reptilian eggs, bigger even than the eggs of the ostriches of Kush. There were also what appeared to be undigested human bones—here a skull, there a jawbone, elsewhere a pelvis.

As Conan dashed into the chamber, followed by the three pursuing dragons, the six in the wheel formation in the center broke off their vigil to lower their heads and stare with eyes like great, green jewels. As their sluggish reptilian brains registered the fact that here was more meat, they turned and started toward the Cimmerian, the claws on the ends of their long-toed, splayed feet scraping over the floor with each lurching stride, and their huge tails swishing from side to side.

To Conan's right gaped the mouth of another tunnel. He ran toward it, but as he reached it the sight of two pairs of great green eyes and the slither of scales on stone halted him. He perceived that two more dragons, aroused by the noise, were coming to investigate. And this tunnel was not wide enough for him to dodge past them.

Next, he made a dash for the bronze doors. But these proved to have no latch or handle on the inside, nor did they yield to his pushing.

The dragons were pouring down upon him, now. He found himself facing a semicircle of the brutes. Sweat ran down his forehead and stung his eyes.

This was worse than the rats. They at least were warm-blooded mammals—his remote kin, according to some philosophers—but these titanic, sluggish saurians were at the opposite end of the scale from man. They were slithering monsters from the primal slime, leftovers from youth of the world, when the earth had shaken to the tread of their even mightier forebears, millions of years before the first man thought to stand erect on his hindlegs and fight for a dominating place in Nature's world.

On they came, like living nightmares from some hideous Hell.

XVII. A Day of Blood and Fire

> The glassy knife bestrews a rain of blood
>   to slake the ghoulish thirst,
> Yet still It hastens on the curst and gory
>   ministers of pain.
>   —*The Visions of Epemitreus*

UNDER THE blazing noonday sun, the line of silent men shuffled slowly toward the mighty pyramid of black-and-scarlet stone. In the fierce heat, Sigurd felt the trickle of sweat down his face and torso.

He had never thought that his end would come in such a scene of barbaric grandeur. On some burning deck, slippery with the blood of the fallen, perhaps—or in the rubble-choked alleys of a seaport under sack, where the flames of burning temples painted the skies with crimson. Or perchance in a desperate duel with some swaggering freebooter in red, roaring Tortage—the cold kiss of a blade against his flesh, the steel sliding in between his ribs, a swart, bearded face grinning into his as red mists rose to drown his vision. But nothing like this!

He gazed about the sunbaked square. On all four sides

of this forum rose tiers of stone benches, and on these benches sat thousands of the richer classes among the Antillians, brave in gold and jade and feathers. The common folk, mainly clad in simple loincloths, stood about the square between the benches and the base of the pyramid. The Antillians stood or sat in tense silence, absorbed in the somber spectacle taking place on top of the pyramid.

At the base of the pyramid, the priesthood of Ptahuacan stood in swaying ranks. Their voices rose like distant waves in a slow, antiphonal song, punctuated by the rumble of huge drums bound in human hide, which thumped and throbbed like the beating of a gigantic heart. The drummers sat in a bay in the side of the pyramid. The vertical walls of this recess were covered with white plaster, on which were painted bright-colored likenesses of the gods and demons of this exotic land.

Sigurd looked up. High above the throng, silhouetted in black against the azure sky, the hierarch, wrapped in his robe of gleaming emerald feathers and gesticulating skywards with gaunt, bare brown arms, sat on a lofty throne to one side of the platform atop the pyramid. The throne glittered blindingly with gems and mother-of-pearl.

On the platform before the throne stood an altar of shiny black stone. The small temple on the pyramid faced the hierarch's throne across the altar. Around the altar, a sacrificial priest and several assistants were at work. Otherwise stripped to loincloth and sandals, the sacrificer wore a fantastically plumed headdress, whose golden bangles splintered the sunrays into dazzling wheels of light and which hid his head.

At this instant, a slave woman was undergoing the ancient Atlantean rite. While the assistants, gripping her bare brown limbs, held her supine upon the altar, the obsidian blade flashed in the sun as it descended. A moment later, the sacrificer's hand held aloft a dripping heart.

Sigurd's jaw dropped; for, even as he watched, the

Feaster on the Pyramid came into view. It materialized out of empty air.

A shadow dimmed the sun. A cold gloom fell over the square. The air bit with the chill of interstellar space. Hovering over the zikkurat, the Demon of Darkness took shape.

Behind him, Sigurd heard a mutter of prayers from the pirates, who were not otherwise a notably pious crew.

Above the pyramid, the Thing solidified and thickened, like darkness with weight and shape, or like a shadow with substance and form. From it a cold, fetid wind blew unceasingly. It looked like a black cloud that had taken the shape of some amorphous sea creature. Its roiling center was fringed with lazily unfolding veils of shadow-stuff. It seethed and swirled like the legendary Maelstrom, supposed to gyrate somewhere off the Arctic coasts of Sigurd's Vanaheim.

Rapt with fascination and dread, Sigurd watched the Thing. It held his gaze with hypnotic fixity, as the cold eye of the serpent was fabled to fascinate the passing bird.

With a chill of horror, the old seafarer realized that this thing of darkness fed upon the life-force released from the bodies of the sacrificial victims. Somehow it drank up and put to use the vitality released by the knives of the red-armed priests. He watched as the high priest fed it, lifting heart after heart toward the smoky cloud.

Then, too, Sigurd realized the meaning of the cryptic symbolism of the ancient Atlanteans. Their emblem of the Black Kraken, which the simple thought to represent a mere giant devilfish, actually depicted this pulsing, growing, black cloud of terror. He remembered the symbol of the Black Kraken that had adorned the prow of the green Antillian galley, which they had destroyed on their way to this accursed isle. The Black Kraken was Xotli, the Demon of Darkness, whereof the old myths whispered!

Sigurd grimly squared his jaw, but within him his courage withered. Had he but guessed the secret hidden behind that grim symbolism, never would he have come so blithely hither on this rash voyage, to end atop a blood-soaked altar beneath a hovering, vampiric Thing from beyond.

One by one, the line of silent men dully shuffled forward. The steep stone stair that led up the side of the zikkurat grew nearer and nearer. Above, the hovering shape of darkness pulsed. It grew larger and larger, darker and darker.

Strangely, none of the sacrificial victims so much as tried to escape. They stood in line with heads bowed or thrown back to stare upwards, shuffling forward. A dull, drugged weariness hung over their spirits.

Not that a break for freedom would have accomplished anything. They were chained at neck and wrist with unbreakable glass bonds and guarded by lines of wary brown warriors with whips and glass-bladed pikes and swords. Lethargically, they moved like sheep to the slaughter.

Perhaps it was some psychic force exerted by the demon above, or some enchantment cast over them by the swaying chorus of priests, who stared up with glazed eyes and slack jaws at their demon-god. Whatever the reason, none sought to elude the bloody knife, which endlessly rose and fell beneath the shadow of the watchful cloud.

Body after body, its chest a gory hole and its limbs flopping, was dragged from the altar stone and dropped by acolytes into the dark mouth of a shaft, which opened to one side of the top of the pyramid. As this was done, a new sacrifice was seized. Four priests took hold of his limbs. A fifth unlocked his bonds, while the sacrificer leaned over to dedicate the victim's life to Xotli. The knife-bearing arm rose and fell; the blood fountained; the heart was held up; another flopping corpse was dragged away to the mouth of the well.

At the head of the line of the pirates, Sigurd, as he

slowly climbed the stair, did not regret being the first to go. Since Conan had gone, the responsibilities of command had fallen to him; and it behooved the chief to set an example of grim courage to his men.

At last came Sigurd's turn. The black vortex was terribly near. He could feel its cold radiance, and deep in his soul he sensed the probing gaze of its hidden eye, lusting for his life and manhood.

The masked priests confronted him. They were stripped to the waist; their lean, brown torsos were splashed with crimson. Their talon-like hands sank into his flesh as they dragged his ponderous bulk across the wet stone. Their eyes were glazed and dull, their look withdrawn.

Lying on his back and staring up at the hovering darkness, Sigurd heard the click as his manacles and neck-ring were unlocked. Hard claws clutched his wrists and ankles. Now the sacrificer came into view, his face masked by a carven devil's head, leering out of a mass of brilliant emerald feathers. The gaunt, bloodsoaked arm reached down to mark his hairy chest. Then the other hand rose into sight, clutching the haft of the glassy knife. The arm swung up against the ebon mass. It started down . . .

Then it stopped. In a hissing puff, Sigurd expelled the breath he had unconsciously held.

The priest stood stiffly against the sky, his plumed head turned like that of a startled hawk. Strange sounds came up to Sigurd from below—sounds like the thunder of an enormous bell, tolling notes of doom. From his throne, the hierarch stopped his incantation to shout down a question.

Then came a loud rustle, as if all the Antillians had sucked in their breath at once. This was followed by an outburst of shrieks.

The sacrificial priest wavered, staring downward at something in the square below. Sigurd heard a deep, groaning, sonorous bellow—a sound like the grunt of a bull crocodile in one of the coastal rivers of Kush, but longer and louder.

The four priests holding Sigurd released his limbs to gawk at the spectacle below, snatching at one another's arms, pointing, and gabbling excitedly. As they did so, the pirates snapped out of their trancelike state. Whether this resulted from the sudden cessation of the hymns wafting up from below, or from the distraction of the archpriest's attention, or even from the wavering of the concentration of the black thing above, none could say. But, whatever the cause, the hypnotic spell that bound them was shattered.

Sigurd rolled off the sacrificial altar. Yasunga, white teeth flashing in his black face, swung his heavy manacles in a glittering curve, which caught the distracted sacrificer on the side of the head and hurled him, bleeding and unconscious, to the pavement.

Meanwhile Sigurd, thinking faster than he ever had in his life, hurled himself upon the priest who held the keys to the manacles. The northerner's hairy hands fastened upon the scrawny neck. As he bore the befeathered figure to the ground, his fingers dug into the priest's throat and shut off his windpipe.

XVIII. Gates of Doom

They lift the gory, dripping fruit before
   the seething ebon cloud;
The silent and adoring crowd is numb,
   bewildered, dazed, and mute.
       —*The Visions of Epemitreus*

SPRINGING FORWARD, Conan swung his long stone club with the courage of desperation. With a thud, it caught the foremost of the giant reptiles on its scaly snout. The stalactite broke in half with a loud crack, and the thick end fell to the ground with a thump.

Hissing furiously, the dragon started back, baring its fangs and lashing its tail. In all the centuries that it had dwelt under Ptahuacan, never had one of its victims turned upon it, let alone given it a painful clout on the nose. The dragon was out of practice at overcoming live prey, and Conan's blow astonished and bewildered its small, reptilian mind as much as it angered it.

Conan's weapon was now reduced to a two-foot spike of limestone. Still, he thought, it was sharp enough to thrust into one of the great, green eyes that blinked at him from the semicircle of scaly heads. And if he could thrust it up to the end, it might reach the sluggish little brain behind the eye. Not, he knew, that this would save him; for such creatures took a long time to realize that they were dead.

But, at least, the dragons would know they had been in a fight. As a couple of the giant lizards hitched themselves closer—practically within snapping distance—Conan rose on the balls of his feet, holding the spike like a dagger. In an instant he would hurt himself at the head of the nearest dragon . . .

Then came an interruption. Down through the shaft in the ceiling, whence came the beam of light that shone down upon a spot of floor and illumined the entire chamber, something fell, to land with a thud on the illuminated spot. It was a naked corpse, whose chest cavity gaped with a huge, ghastly wound.

Grunting, the dragon that Conan had struck wheeled around and waddled quickly over to the corpse. Such unresisting food was more to its taste than creatures that gave it a rap on the nose, merely because it tried to eat them. As the first dragon turned away, another and then another imitated its action, until they were all brainlessly streaming away across the cavern floor.

As the first dragon reached the corpse, it scooped the upper part of the dead man's body up into its vast jaws, turning its head sideways to do so. But, as it raised its head, a second dragon grabbed the dangling legs of the corpse. The two reptiles engaged in a grisly tug-of-war, grunting and wagging their massive heads from side to side, while others crowded round, trying to snatch a piece of the corpse.

Presently, the body tore in half with a rending sound. The two dragons that had first seized it backed away to gulp down their portions, while the others scrambled for the entrails that had spilled out on the ground.

In a flash of insight, Conan understood much that had

puzzled him. For one thing, he had wondered what such huge flesh-eaters could find to live on in this maze of caverns. Bats and luminous grubs would surely not sustain them, but a steady supply of sacrificial victims would support them in draconian luxury. The girl Catlaxoc and the arch-thief Metemphoc had both described the mass sacrifices to Xotli, and the corpses had to be disposed of somehow. This arrangement explained the fact that, when he had first entered the cavern, Conan had found a half-dozen dragons crouched in a circle beneath the shaft, with heads expectantly raised.

Then, too, Conan realized what must have happened to him. His travels through this underground realm had taken him round in a circle. He had originally planned to emerge from the subterranean labyrinth under the Vestibule of the Gods. This grim gray edifice rose on the square of the temple pyramid, and in it the slaves and captives destined for sacrifice, including his own crew, were held.

Instead, the battle with the rats had driven him off his course, and his fall into the underground river had resulted in his being carried still farther away from his memorized route. But some whim of fate or of the gods had brought him around in a loop, returning him at length to the place he first meant to reach, or at least very near it.

The falling body, Conan was sure, was part of the exhausted surplus of the sacrifice, in which hearts were torn from living victims. The shaft down which the corpse had fallen probably extended up through the pyramid to an opening near the top. Therefore, he reasoned, he must be directly beneath the pyramid—or at least under the square surrounding it.

All this flashed through Conan's mind in the space of three heartbeats. As the monsters turned away from him, he dashed around the perimeter of the chamber to the vertical ladder, made of pegs driven into holes in the wall, which led from the floor of the cave up to the platform on which the Antillian guard was stationed. This guard no longer lounged lethargically; he pointed at Conan with astonishment and shouted unintelligible questions.

Conan reached the foot of the ladder. The guard was armed, and it would not be easy to climb to the platform in the face of his weapons. But then a dragon, who had failed to get a piece in the scramble for the corpse, turned back toward Conan, its long, forked tongue flicking out. Conan decided to chance the guard rather than again face the horde of giant lizards.

With the speed of a monkey scrambling out of the way of a lion, Conan went up the ladder. By the time the first of the reptiles had reached its foot, he was twenty feet up, well out of their reach.

Next, he had to cope with the guard. He drew the dirk from the sheath at his back and put the blade between his teeth. Then he resumed his climb.

Soon he found himself staring up into the astonished brown face of the guard, who squatted at the edge of his platform. The man jabbered at Conan and threateningly waved his glass-bladed sword.

Holding a rung just out of the guard's reach with his left hand, Conan hooked a knee around a rung to give himself purchase. Then he took the dirk from between his teeth. Closing one eye to sight on the guard's form, he brought his right arm slowly back—then sharply forward. The dirk flashed through the air, struck the guard in the hollow at the base of his throat, and buried itself halfway to the hilt.

With a choking gurgle, the guard staggered to his feet. He dropped his sword with a clatter to clutch at the blade buried in his throat. Then he teetered forward and plunged off the platform. Conan had to fend off his falling body to keep from being knocked off the ladder himself. The guard struck the floor of the chamber with a thud. A strangled shriek was cut off by the crunch of a pair of dragon's jaws. From below, sounds of another reptilian feast wafted up.

Breathing hard, Conan hauled himself up to the platform and sat down on the edge with his booted feet dangling. The last hour had seen him through some of the closest calls of an adventurous life.

Some dragons remained at the foot of the ladder, gazing hopefully up at him. Little by little they trailed away. Those that had failed to fill their bellies from the recent windfalls resumed their circle around the bright spot in the center of the floor. Presently, with a whistle and a thump, another mutilated corpse fell down the shaft, to be pounced upon and squabbled over by the scaly reception committee.

Having recovered from his exertions, Conan got up and explored. Behind the platform was a tunnel closed by a bronze grille. Beyond the grille, steps led up into the gloom. The grille opened at Conan's touch. Inside this gate was a large recess in the wall, and in this recess a gigantic bronze wheel was mounted. The spokes projected beyond the rim to form handles, so that it resembled, on a larger scale, one of the tiller wheels that Conan had seen on large Zingaran galleons. The wheel was thick with the green, waxy coating of verdigris. It must have stood there for ages since last being turned.

Conan frowned in thought. His gaze wandered to the huge bronze doors across the chamber, beyond the circle of ghoulishly waiting dragons. Why should those doors have been put there in the first place? They must have cost the folk of Ptahuacan a tremendous lot of labor to install. Presumably, a passage led from the other side of them to the world above. But all they were good for was to loose the horde of dragons upon the citizens. Why should the hierarch wish any such thing?

The answer came to Conan's mind with a snap. The

dragons served a double purpose. Not only did they dispose of the remains of the sacrificial victims, but also they served as a last-ditch secret weapon, in case the downtrodden populace should rise in rebellion against the priesthood.

And how were they opened? Conan could not be sure, but his glance strayed back to the ancient bronze wheel.

Out in the square, the sacrifice to Xotli must be taking place. Perhaps it had been going on for hours. The square would be packed with people, with the place of honor, nearest to the dragon gates, reserved for the priestly hierarchy. A glorious plan took form in Conan's brain . . .

Conan stepped through the grille and confronted the wheel. He drew a deep breath, set his burly shoulders to it, and put a surge of strength behind it. Metal groaned under pressure. Conan's boots slid and grated on the stone floor.

He relaxed, took several deep breaths, and tried again. The sinews writhed across his back and shoulders. Somewhere on the other side of the wall, tortured metal squeaked and groaned. Dust and dislodged particles of dirt pattered down. The wheel moved a fingerbreadth, then a fingerbreadth more, with a shriek of metal forced into motion after aeons of inactivity.

Again Conan strained at the wheel, gripping the spokes so fiercely that it almost seemed as if his white-knuckled fingers would sink into the bronze. He heaved until the blood pounded in his temples and roared in his ears. The wheel lurched and revolved several inches. Within the wall somewhere, ponderous counterweights boomed into motion.

Across the chamber, a crack of light appeared between the valves of the great bronze door.

Another heave, and the motion of the wheel became suddenly easier. From beyond the wall came the growl and rumble of the ancient mechanism, forced into motion after so many quiet centuries.

The crack between the doors widened. With a clank of engaging machinery, the wheel began to spin of its own accord, faster and faster. The valves of the bronze door swung wide on screaming hinges. The dragons, which had been peering and shuffling about uneasily as these unaccustomed noises came to their ears, turned toward the opening doors.

Beyond the doors, a steep ramp led up, then turned sharply out of sight. Light came down from above—good, strong daylight. Conan inferred that another pair of doors at the top of the ramp had opened at the same time. These must be in the base of the pyramid or in one of the buildings surrounding the square.

As Conan, gasping for breath, collapsed over the wheel, the dragons, emitting excited bellows, waddled through the open doors. With claws scraping and slipping on the ramp, they poured up the slope and out of sight. From the dark mouths of the tunnels that opened into the chamber, more dragons appeared, roused from their long slumbers by the noise of the mechanism and the roars of their fellows. These joined the procession up the ramp, until forty-odd of the creatures had passed out of sight on their way to the upper world whence a sudden chorus of horrified shrieks wafted faintly down into the chamber.

Still panting, Conan lay against the bottom of the bronze wheel, waiting for his heart to slow down from its wild pounding and smiling grimly through his stiff, gray beard.

XIX. The Crystal Talisman

The horror from the primal slime lived on
  to slake its fiendish lust,
When bright Atlantis fell to dust beneath
  the trampling hooves of time.
                    —*The Visions of Epemitreus*

As CONAN heaved on the great bronze wheel in the passage below the square of the pyramid, a crack appeared in the painted plaster that covered the vertical wall of the bay in the side of the pyramid. The plaster broke into fragments which showered down on the pavement at the feet of the drumming, chanting priests. The bronze doors, which the plaster had masked, groaned and squealed as they swung slowly outwards, even as their mates, the similar doors in the chamber of the dragons below, were opening.

The chant died away to silence as the priests backed away from the opening door valves. They stared at one another; questions flew back and forth. Behind the priests, the thousands of Antillians, from the humble artisans standing in the square to the nobility on the tiers of benches, also shifted uneasily. They stood on tiptoe, peered, and questioned.

On top of the pyramid, the sacrificer paused in the midst of his sacrifices, just as he was about to decardiate the stout foreign ruffian with the graying reddish beard. He leaned over and shouted down a question, which was lost in the gathering hubbub.

A trememdous hiss came from the dark interior behind the opening doors. Out into the sunlight shambled the first of the dragons to reach the top of the ramp—fifty feet of slate-gray scales, waddling briskly on bowed, muscular legs and splayed, long-toed feet. Its raised head swiveled from side to side as its great, green eyes, their pupils contracted to slits by the glare, took in the scene around it. From the tip of its long, crocodilian snout, a yard of pink, forked tongue flicked out.

Screaming, the ranks of the chanting priests broke. The priests fought their way into the crowd of common Antillians, who in turn surged away from the doors. In the panic push, men and women were thrown down and the life was trampled out of them.

One priest tripped on his feathered robe and fell. Before he could recover, the jaws of the dragon slammed shut upon him. The reptile raised its head. Then it jerked its head back several times, while the elastic skin of its throat swelled and shrank with gulping motions. With each jerk, the priest slid further into its jaws, until only his feet, still wearing their gilded stilt shoes, were visible. A final jerk and gulp, and the dragon's throat bulged as its prey slid down its gullet.

Meanwhile other dragons, with tongues flickering and jaws opening to emit their groaning roars, crowded past the first. There seemed to be no end to the procession. They scrambled across the pavement and plunged into the screaming, clawing mass of Antillians. Some people were crushed beneath the monsters' clawed feet; others were

172

knocked about like dolls by casual swings of huge, scaly tails. Blood lay in puddles and ran into the gutters in sticky scarlet streams. Everywhere, dragons paused to raise their heads and gulp down their prey before plunging on after another mouthful.

Meanwhile, high up on the side of the red-and-black pyramid, a small door opened. Conan stepped out, carrying the sword of black glass with which the guard had been armed. The salt wind from the sea whipped his shaggy gray mane. He expanded his huge chest to take in a lungful of clean, fresh air, welcome after the stenches of the charnel cavern world below.

After he had opened the gates that loosed the reptilian horde upon the people of Ptahuacan, he had mounted the stone stair that slanted up from the platform in the wall of the dragon chamber. Other passages branched off horizontally from this tunnel. But Conan, reasoning that the sacrifice should be taking place on top of the pyramid and that the steepest passageway would bring him out closest to that place, continued on up, until he had come to the door from which he just emerged.

For an instant he stood staring down, watching with grim satisfaction the scene of havoc and madness below. Some of the dragons had reached the tiers of stone benches where the nobles and higher priests had sat. They were lurching up and down these benches, pursuing and capturing screaming, befeathered fugitives.

From his height, Conan could see along the streets that let out of the square. Each of these streets now bore a stream of madly running fugitives. Some darted into the first open door they reached, to slam and bar it against later arrivals. Others kept running until they passed through the city gates and straggled out into the countryside.

Craning his neck in the other direction, Conan looked

up to the top of the pyramid. Here, where rose the temple of Xotli, knots of men struggled. The colors of their skins told Conan that some of these were his own crew, battling with priests and guards.

Then Conan became aware of a figure standing near him on one of the stairways that led to the top of the pyramid. This was the gaunt old hierarch himself, recognizable by the splendor of his feathered robe—now torn—and his golden ornaments. His plumed headpiece was gone, and blood ran down one side of his head. Leaning forward, he gesticulated frantically with his skinny brown arms, screaming commands to the milling soldiers and priests below.

At the base of the pyramid directly below the hierarch, one of the dragons looked up, its pink tongue feeling the air. Then the monster began to claw its way up the stair.

A wicked grin wrinkled Conan's bearded face. Thrusting his glass sword through his belt, he vaulted to the next higher level of the yard-high steps that made up the pyramid. He stepped softly along the step until he came to the stair on which the hierarch stood, behind and above that personage. Without a word, he placed both hands on the small of the archpriest's back and gave a terrific shove.

The hierarch shot out from the surface of the pyramid in an arc and struck the steps lower down. He rolled over and over in a whirl of brown limbs and green feathers, until he reached the dragon coming up from below. A loud chomp, and the jaws closed upon the age-old master of Antillia.

The high priest's skull-like head jerked frantically; his bony fists beat futilely against the scaly jaws. Then, as one of the saber-like fangs reached a vital organ, the body relaxed. The high priest's screams ceased; his head and limbs hung limply. Squatting at the base of the pyramid, the dragon settled down to the agreeable task of swallowing its catch whole.

Up on top of the pyramid, Yasunga still swung his chains like a flail, while sweat ran down his ebony hide. Another pirate and a priest rolled over and over on the pavement, hands locked on each other's throats. Milo the boatswain had tangled a soldier's halberd in his chains and strove to hold the weapon down, while the soldier struggled to wrench it loose. Artanes the Zamorian fought two Antillians at once with a captured pike, which he wielded like a quarterstaff. Sigurd struggled to unlock the manacles and neck-rings of some of the pirates, while others fended off the attempts of a few priests and soldiers to get to him and recover the keys. Many of the Antillians had fled from the top of the pyramid, but some still struggled with their former captives.

With a booming war cry, Conan bounded up the steps and hurled himself into the fray. In his mail shirt, he was easily a match for any three of the little brown men. An Antillian head went flying from its body to bounce and roll down the steps of the pyramid. Another man of Ptahuacan collapsed in a mess of spilled entrails. Another clutched, screaming, at the stump of a hand.

Their eyes big with superstitious terror, the Antillians gave back before Conan, who lunged hither and thither like a razor-edged whirlwind, constantly shifting his position so that it was hard for an opponent to get a good cut or thrust at him. If he was not so agile as he had been decades before, his attack was still the most awesome thing the Antillians had ever seen.

"A demon! He is a demon!" they cried, backing away.

Soon nobody stood between Conan, bloody glass sword in hand, and the knot around Sigurd. The Northman looked up.

"Amra!" roared Sigurd. "By Crom and Mitra and all the gods, we thought you dead!"

"Not yet, Redbeard! I still have some killing to do."

175

Conan clapped the stout Vanr on one shoulder. "What's here?"

"I'm trying to get these damned rings unlocked, but it takes an expert touch. Can you do it faster, ere they rush us again?"

"The key's too slow," growled Conan. "Let's see if glass will cut glass. Stretch that chain across the altar stone."

The glass of the swords and that of the chains, he thought, were basically the same material. But, just as the steel of a sword is more finely tempered than the iron of an ordinary chain, so the glass of his sword might be superior to that of the glass chains. Whereas a chain must merely hold, a sword must cut. Well, he would put it to the test.

His sword flashed in the afternoon sun as he swung it above his iron-gray head. The blade whistled down, with all the power of his huge muscles behind it, to strike the altar surface with a crash. A link of the chain shattered beneath the blow, the flying shards sparkling like diamonds.

"Now the next!" cried Conan.

Chain after chain was severed, until all the pirates who were still chained were free. As they were released, they looked around for dropped weapons to snatch up before plunging back into the fray. The remaining priests and soldiers on the top of the pyramid fled with cries of despair, abandoning still more weapons to their attackers.

Conan looked below. The unleashed monsters had proved an effective diversion, engaging the attention of most of the Antillians and enabling Conan to free his shipmates while the number of enemies still on top of the pyramid was too small to interfere.

The square was now mostly clear. Here and there a dragon lumbered about the pavement, chasing a scampering fugitive. The soldiers who had not fled in the general exodus stood in solid clumps, forming hedgehogs of leveled spears to hold off the dragons. Priests moved among the soldiers, directing and exhorting them.

Most of the dragons, too, had fled the square. All had fed—some several times over—and their present desire was to find a quiet spot to sink into digestive torpor. Some lurched along the streets of the city after the fleeing multitudes, out through the gates and across the cornfields and vegetable gardens of the Antillians. Some plodded down to the harbor, slipped into the water, and swam with serpentine undulations along the coast. Even as Conan watched, the last pair of dragons waddled out of the square.

The priests now began directing the soldiers remaining in the square, and putting them into formation. Some priests pointed to the top of the pyramid and shouted to others, urging an attack on the pirates. Soon, several hundred little brown warriors had been formed into ranks and files, facing the pyramid from all sides. Several soldiers trotted into the square, lugging baskets full of the Antillians' glass globes containing the soporific gas.

Conan's eyes narrowed in grim estimation. Now that the dragons were no longer fighting on the side of the pirates, he did not doubt that the well-drilled hosts of Ptahuacan would give a good account of themselves. Perhaps this square would see the end of him and his band. At least, the gods would be treated to one hell of a magnificent last stand.

"Can we break them, Lion?" rumbled Sigurd. He slapped his bare chest and hefted a crystal cutlass. "Bowels of Nergal and breasts of Ishtar, but I be spoiling for a fight with those little brown bastards! After days in the stinking jakes they call a dungeon, feeding on cold swill, 'twill delight me to smash a few heads and rip out a few guts ere I fall. Say the word, comrade; we all be ready!"

Conan nodded, his eyes smoldering. He was about to

177

lift his sword and lead the corsairs in one last, glorious charge down the stairs of the pyramid, to burst through those glittering ranks or go down before the glass-bladed weapons . . .

But an ominous shadow fell upon him. He looked up into the hovering, swirling cloud of blackness that was the Demon from Beyond.

Crom! How could he have forgotten this evil thing from the spaces between the stars? The gory ritual that had summoned it into this world, from whatever unholy dimension it dwelt in, had given it shape and substance within this realm of matter. Even the disruption of the ceremony, while it may have weakened the being, had not dissolved its physical existence or broken the mighty spells that gave it life in the world of man.

It had clung, brooding, above the scenes of tumult and slaughter, viewing with cold malignancy the destruction of the Antillians and the freeing of the victims destined for its supernatural feast. Now its inhuman intelligence had moved it into action. As it hung, pulsing, above the pirate crew, it sent tentacles of mental force probing downward from its dark, turbulent center.

To Conan, it was as if icy, impalpable fingers pierced the secret places of his mind, pawing through his memories like a freebooter ransacking a temple in some conquered city. He felt the touch of alien thoughts, penetrating the roots of his inmost soul. All his vigorous manhood rebelled against this mental violation.

In the strangest battle of his life, he fought against the mind-probing tendrils of darkness. Here in this realm of thought, mind alone battled against mind. No plate armor of tempered steel or shield of iron-bound oak and tanned bull's hide could resist, no iron blade or muscular arm could repel the mental tentacles that insinuated themselves into his brain.

Conan felt these searching antennae fingering and deadening the power centers of his brain, so that an icy numbness spread over his body. Little by little, his limbs lost their strength until he could barely stand.

But he fought on, grimly clinging to life and consciousness with all the ferocious tenacity of his primitive background. Never had he thought of using his mind thus as a weapon. Yet he was conscious of his mind's lashing out in a mental struggle with the insidious, gliding tendrils of the alien intelligence that sought to destroy his life course. He felt his mind strike out at the slithering tentacles of the mind called Xotli, tearing them loose from his centers of mental energy.

With deadly swiftness, the other worldly mind turned to a different kind of attack. Its tentacles attacked the centers of his physical consciousness and began draining vital energy from him. His sight dimmed; his consciousness blurred. The white plaster on the front of the little temple atop the pyramid turned yellow, and invisible bells rang in his ears. He felt himself slipping away, falling down a well into cold blackness . . .

But still he fought on, striving to shield his mind from the thing that sucked the life force from him.

In the roaring whirlpool of his struggling mind, a dim wisp of memory rose to the turbulent surface of his consciousness. He recalled standing in spirit form in the black heart of Mount Golamira, while the splendid specter of the sage Epemitreus spoke to him. Once more he heard the voice of the ancient philosopher, whispering:

And one gift alone I may give you. Bear it through every trial, for in your hour of greatest need it will be your salvation. Nay, I can tell you naught more. In time of need, your heart will tell you how to use this talisman.

Dimly, Conan remembered the coldly glittering thing he had found in his hand upon awakening from the prophetic dream, in the silence of his royal bedchamber—the jeweled talisman he had worn on a silver chain about his neck ever since, through all his subsequent adventures.

The strength had drained from his huge limbs, but he still bore within him the unquenchable vitality that had brought him through so many deadly perils in the course of his long and action-filled life. Now, in this hour of his greatest peril on earth, he called upon his hidden resources.

One massive, scarred hand rose to his throat, pulled the crystal phoenix out from beneath his mail shirt, and broke the chain with a jerk.

As a black vise closed about his brain, he dropped the talisman. Dimly, he heard it tinkle on the stone.

With his last ounce of consciousness, as his mind spun into a whirling void, he brought his booted heel down upon the amulet and crushed it into powder. Then he pitched forward into blackness.

XX. Gods of Light and Darkness

And when you face the Kraken's might, that on
   the sacrifice has fled,
Stand fast, where other men have fled, and let
   the crystal phoenix smite!
                    —*The Visions of Epemitreus*

FROM SOME vast distance, across nighted gulfs of cold
and darkness, a far, faint voice was calling him . . .

As consciousness returned to Conan's brain, sensation
filtered back into his body. He felt horny hands clutching
him and rough stone scraping against his dragging legs.
He gasped for air, choked, and opened bewildered eyes, to
find himself supported between the wheezing hulk of Sigurd Redbeard on one side and the turbaned form of Goram Singh on the other.

"Set me down, in Crom's name," he grunted. "I can
walk by myself."

They stopped and helped him to stand. "I think so, anyway," he grumbled, as his numb limbs folded under him.
He would have pitched forward down the slope of the pyramid if his comrades had not caught him and propped him
up again.

They sat him down on one of the steps of the stone stair that led up the face of the pyramid. Conan felt a million hot needles in his limbs as circulation returned. He looked around, gathering his faculties.

A huge, strange silence reigned over the scene. His men had dragged him halfway down the stair to the base of the pyramid. At the base, ranks of guards were drawn up. But the small brown warriors in glittering glass armor paid no heed to the pirates. With staring eyes and expressions of awe and terror, they gaped upward

Turning to look back and up over his shoulder, Conan felt his marrow freeze. High above them all, over the temple atop the black-and-scarlet pyramid, a strange force pulsed, flickered, and grew.

"It came from the jewel you crushed underfoot," muttered Sigurd, casting an uneasy glance upward. "Mitra only knows what's happening up yonder, but we all seemed to hear an inward voice, warning us to get away, and that right speedily. Sink me for a lubber, but all this devilish magic and witchery gets a simple fighting man down!"

Conan chuckled. Far above, a diamond-like dust of sparkling, shimmering light rose in gusts and whorls from the pulverized remains of the crystal talisman. The black cloud of Xotli still hung above the altar stone, its tendrils of dark, smoky stuff stirring and questing uneasily, as if it sensed the approach of a deadly foe.

The spinning motes of light rose and brightened, becoming a whirling galaxy of blazing brilliance. Spiral arms scintillated against the dark mass of Xotli like millions of stars against the dark of night.

Conan shivered, as if his hair had been ruffled by the icy winds that blow between the stars. A shape of light took form, sprang erect, and folded Xotli into a many-tentacled embrace. Mitra—for somehow Conan knew that this was indeed the god—spoke. The thunder of a thousand tempests boomed and rolled about the square of the pyramid. The earth shook, and the pyramid itself moved under the pirates' feet, bringing down a mass of masonry. With a deafening roar, a large section of the square caved in and dropped out of sight, carrying hundreds of shrieking little brown soldiers with it and sending up a blinding, choking cloud of dust. Conan realized that this must be the collapse of the cavern of the dragons.

"Get out!" roared Conan.

He lurched to his feet and stumbled down the remaining steps to the bottom of the stair. After him poured the howling pirates, those already armed in front. But, at the bottom, they found no foe to face them. The ranks of the Antillian soldiery had dissolved in rout. Dropping their glass-bladed weapons, the brown warriors were racing for the gates of the city, throwing aside their crystal helms and mail shirts to run faster. Only their dwindling backs were to be seen, and those not for long.

"Grab these weapons!" yelled Conan. "Then to the harbor!"

Far above, the gods of light and darkness were locked in battle. Fiery blasts of lightning crackled from the whirling, starry form of light, about which tentacles of dark smoke also writhed and clutched.

The earth quivered underfoot. Across the square, the huge gray Vestibule of the Gods came crashing down in a slow landslide of rubble, soon hidden from sight in a vast cloud of dust. Like a giant tree felled by a woodsman, a tall, tapering tower leaned, buckled, and slammed to earth, making the ground beneath the pirates' feet jump.

Conan led his men on a jog-trot through the streets of Ptahuacan, paying no heed to the few Antillians they passed. The latter, in a frenzy of terror, likewise ignored the escaping captives in their own frantic efforts to save themselves.

"This way!" roared Conan. "To the harbor, before the whole damned city falls on us!"

Behind them, the shadows of afternoon lengthened in the pyramid square, now and then lit by a blaze of brilliance brighter than the noonday sun. The sounds of the supernatural combat crackled, boomed, roared, growled, and thundered. Before shafts of intolerable light, the black cloud seemed to fold in upon itself. It shrank, dissipated—and died.

The tension of supernatural forces that held it together was released. As these forces failed, the city shook like the head of a beaten drum, and more buildings crumbled. The square of the pyramid vanished. In its place, a ball of fire, many times brighter than the sun, blazed for an instant and was gone with a thunderclap that temporarily deafened every human being within the city.

A stupendous column of thick, black smoke arose over the broken city, mushrooming upward. The starry lightnings of the god of light played for an instant about its top like a supernal crown. Then these, too faded, and the smoky column began to disperse, mingling with the gray cloud of dust that hung over the city. Here and there, darker smoke rose from a burning house.

Little by little, Ptahuacan crept back to life. Its people trickled back from the countryside. But, on their return, they found a surprise.

Most of the priesthood had either been killed in the fall of the temples or had fled out of the city. Within Ptahuacan, during the night and day following the catastrophe, only one man remained at the head of any strong grouping. This was Metemphoc, the master thief.

While the city was nearly empty, his well-disciplined corps of thieves seized the remaining large buildings and the stores of arms. The few priests they found, they slew. The dungeons were thrown open, releasing not only convicted felons of Metemphoc's band but also hundreds of ordinary Antillians who, on one pretext or another, had been jailed to await sacrifice to Xotli. Many of these allied themselves with Metemphoc, although others refused for fear of the priests and their god, or preferred to wait to see which side would prove the stronger.

The priests who had fled the city gathered a small force of warriors still faithful to them and tried to fight their way back into the metropolis. But Conan's band, now fully armed, took them in the rear and sent them fleeing again.

So, under the leadership of fat, crafty old Metemphoc, Ptahuacan settled down to its huge task of repair and rebuilding. The master thief might not prove an ideal ruler; but he could hardly do worse than the priesthood that had held the land in its fearsome grip for so many centuries. And so to this last, lone outpost of the great civilization of old Atlantis, some little time of peace and quiet came.

And perhaps from some unknown realm beyond the stars, the ghosts of those old gods who had reigned in the skies above Atlantis in ages gone, and who had turned upon the island continent at last and plunged her into the depths of the great, green sea when her children abandoned them to worship dark Xotli—perhaps those dead gods saw, and smiled, and—with what little power that remained to them—blessed.

Crom, but it felt good to have a solid deck underfoot again—even a cursed strange deck like this one! After the fall of Ptahuacan, a month and a half before, Conan had eaten and drunk deep. Worn to exhaustion by his struggles through the underworld of Ptahuacan and then in the city itself, he had slept a whole day and two nights through. But in the days that followed, as he loafed and lazed, swapping yarns with his men and eating and drinking enough for three, his old strength crept back.

Now, as dawn painted the East with strokes of crimson and gold, he strode the gilded planking of the dragon ship and drank deeply of the clear, cold, salt breeze, which lifted the gray fog from the green face of the Western Main. He felt a vast contentment. Ha! Old, was he? Time to creep beneath the covers and let mumbling physickers take over, to glide him painlessly into the afterworld?

He snorted. He could still give the woman Catlaxoc a night that left her limp but happy. The old urge to adventure, the old wanderlust, still filled his breast. Enough vitality lingered in his gaunt, towering form for another adventure or two, at least!

He slapped the gilded rail with a firm hand, as a man might clap the flank of a lusty stallion. One last adventure . . .

He gazed about him. With the unerring eye of an old freebooter, Conan had seized the best ship in the harbor when he had burst into the waterfront with his gasping, staggering pack of dust-gray pirates at his heels and half the city falling in ruin behind him. He had herded them aboard this superb craft, the deadliest fighting ship he had ever seen. She had fought the *Red Lion* to a standstill when, months before, she had loomed out of the gray mists like some monster from earth's dawn. He chuckled at the thought of the consternation the weird Atlantean craft would cause back in the Barachas.

Not that his appropriation of this craft, which he named the *Winged Dragon*, had been without difficulties. The pirates, conservative like all sailors, had disliked the strange rig. Why not, they said, pump out the beached hull of the *Red Lion* and put her back into service? But Conan discovered that the *Red Lion* had been too badly damaged to repair and refit without the aid of a shipyard of the lands across the ocean. Her hull had been burnt through in places; her masts and sails and rigging were gone and could be replaced only with enormous effort. It was more practical to salvage her stores of weapons and materials and transfer them to the *Winged Dragon*.

Then many days of practice were needed to familiarize his crew with the exotic rig and to make the changes in the ship that Conan decided upon. Moreover, the *Winged Dragon* was a galley; therefore she required a larger crew than a sailing vessel of the same size. Luckily, there were plenty of adventurous youths among the Antillians who signed on as rowers.

Sigurd Redbeard clumped up the ladder to the poop deck, hawking and spitting. "Ha, Lion!" he grunted. "Sleep well?"

"Like a dead man."

Sigurd shrugged and glanced back to where the seven isles of Antillia were hidden by the morning mists. "There be dead men back there a-plenty," he said. "By the green beard of Lir and Dagon's fish tail, I do admire the way ye stage a prison break!"

"What mean you?" demanded Conan.

"Naught, naught! But a man must needs respect the way ye spring your comrades out of a tight spot—if ye have to lay half the city in ruins to do it."

Conan laughed harshly. "Aye! And I'd gladly lay the other half in ruins to have an old walrus like you beside me."

Sigurd sighed. " 'Tis good of ye to say so, Amra. Me, I'm no longer so limber as once I was." He glanced at the peaks of Antillia, rising out of the mist. "We might have done worse than take up Metemphoc's offer, to let him hire us as his mercenary army."

Conan grinned and shook his head. "We former kings get proud as the devil. We won't serve other men when we can be masters ourselves."

The sun was up, filling the sky with brightness. White gulls circled, squealing, and blue waves slapped the newly tarred and painted hull of the *Winged Dragon*. Conan took another deep breath. Beside him, Sigurd squinted against the brightness of dawn and glanced at his scarred, gray-bearded comrade.

"Whither now, Lion?" he queried. "Back to the Barachas, or to harry the coasts of Stygia and Shem?"

Conan shook his head. "This ship is not made to cross the great gap of ocean. With all these rowers to feed and water, we'd never make it."

"That green galley we first met did."

"Aye, but I'm no sorcerer, to summon up a crew of spirits to ply the oars."

Conan pondered. Old Metemphoc had told him much. Even farther west, at the very rim of the world, the old thief had confided, lay a vast new continent. Mayapan, the Atlanteans and their Antillian descendants had called it. They raided its coasts for gold, emeralds, and virgin copper; for red-skinned slaves and curious birds with gorgeous plumage; for tiger-like cats whose pelts were marked with black rosettes on tawny gold. Here, too, were barbarian states founded by renegades from Atlantis and Antillia, where the cults of the Giant Serpent and of the Saber-toothed Tiger carried on their ferocious rivalry in a welter of human sacrifice and abominable worship.

A new world, he thought; a world of trackless jungles and spacious plains, of towering mountains and hidden lakes, where immense rivers writhed like serpents of molten silver through depths of emerald jungle, where unknown peoples worshiped strange and fearsome gods . . .

What sights and adventures might not await him in the remotenesses of Mayapan? Conan wondered. Metemphoc had called him "Kukulcan," but whether this was a sobriquet in the Antillian tongue, or a corruption of "Conan Cimmerian" or some such phrase, Conan never knew. If he went to this new world, where people had never seen bearded men with weapons of steel and glass—why, he might conquer another vast empire, be worshiped as a god, bring bits of civilization of the old world to the new, and become the hero of legends that would endure ten thousand years . . .

"Crom knows!" he snorted. "Let's break our fast and talk on this matter. Saving the world surely gives one an appetite!"

They went below. A few hours later, the great ship, which the folk of Mayapan were to call *Quetzalcoatl*—meaning "winged (or feathered) serpent" in their uncouth tongue—lifted anchor. She sailed south and then, skirting the Antillian Isles, into the unknown West.

But whither, the ancient chronicle, which endeth here, sayeth not.

CONAN

☐ 11577-2	**CONAN, #1**	$2.50
☐ 11595-0	**CONAN OF CIMMERIA, #2**	$2.50
☐ 11614-0	**CONAN THE FREEBOOTER, #3**	$2.50
☐ 11596-9	**CONAN THE WANDERER, #4**	$2.50
☐ 11634-5	**CONAN THE ADVENTURER, #5**	$2.25
☐ 11599-3	**CONAN THE BUCCANEER, #6**	$2.50
☐ 11616-7	**CONAN THE WARRIOR, #7**	$2.50
☐ 11603-5	**CONAN THE CONQUEROR, #9**	$2.50
☐ 11608-6	**CONAN THE AVENGER, #10**	$2.50
☐ 11612-4	**CONAN OF AQUILONIA, #11**	$2.50
☐ 11613-2	**CONAN OF THE ISLES, #12**	$2.50

Available at your local bookstore or return this form to:

ACE SCIENCE FICTION
P.O. Box 400, Kirkwood, N.Y. 13795

Please send me the titles checked above. I enclose _____.
Include 75¢ for postage and handling if one book is ordered; 50¢ per book for
two to five. If six or more are ordered, postage is free. California, Illinois, New
York and Tennessee residents please add sales tax.

NAME _____

ADDRESS _____

CITY_____ STATE/ZIP_____

Allow six weeks for delivery. A-04

BEST-SELLING
Science Fiction
and
Fantasy

47807-7	**THE LEFT HAND OF DARKNESS,** Ursula K. Le Guin $2.50	
16016-8	**DORSAI!,** Gordon R. Dickson $2.50	
80579-5	**THIEVES' WORLD,** Robert Lynn Asprin, editor $2.75	
11577-2	**CONAN #1.** Robert E. Howard, L. Sprague de Camp, Lin Carter $2.50	
49141-3	**LORD DARCY INVESTIGATES,** Randall Garrett $2.50	
21888-1	**EXPANDED UNIVERSE,** Robert A. Heinlein $3.50	
87325-1	**THE WARLOCK UNLOCKED,** Christopher Stasheff $2.75	
26194-0	**FUZZY PAPERS,** H. Beam Piper $2.95	
05463-3	**BERSERKER,** Fred Saberhagen $2.50	
10257-3	**CHANGELING,** Roger Zelazny $2.50	
51547-9	**THE MAGIC GOES AWAY,** Larry Niven $2.50	

Available at your local bookstore or return this form to:

 ACE SCIENCE FICTION
P.O. Box 400, Kirkwood, N.Y. 13795

Please send me the titles checked above. I enclose _____
Include 75¢ for postage and handling if one book is ordered; 50¢ per book for
two to five. If six or more are ordered, postage is free. California, Illinois, New
York and Tennessee residents please add sales tax.

NAME _____

ADDRESS _____

CITY_____ STATE/ZIP_____

Allow six weeks for delivery.

SF 9

MORE SCIENCE

FICTION!

ADVENTURE